See Me

Blind Sight Series, Volume 1

Lexy Timms

Published by Dark Shadow Publishing, 2020.

SEE ME

First edition. February 13, 2020.

Written by Lexy Timms.

Also by Lexy Timms

A Bad Boy Bullied Romance
I Hate You
I Hate You A Little Bit
I Hate You A Little Bit More

A Burning Love Series
Spark of Passion
Flame of Desire
Blaze of Ecstasy

A Chance at Forever Series
Forever Perfect
Forever Desired
Forever Together

A Dating App Series
I've Been Matched
You've Been Matched

We've Been Matched

A "Kind of" Billionaire
Taking a Risk
Safety in Numbers
Pretend You're Mine

A Maybe Series
Maybe I Should
Maybe I Shouldn't
Maybe I Did

BBW Romance Series
Capturing Her Beauty
Pursuing Her Dreams
Tracing Her Curves

Beating the Biker Series
Making Her His
Making the Break
Making of Them

Billionaire Banker Series
Banking on Him

Price of Passion
Investing in Love
Knowing Your Worth
Treasured Forever
Banking on Christmas

Billionaire Holiday Romance Series
Driving Home for Christmas
The Valentine Getaway
Cruising Love

Billionaire in Disguise Series
Facade
Illusion
Charade

Billionaire Secrets Series
The Secret
Freedom
Courage
Trust
Impulse
Billionaire Secrets Box Set Books #1-3

Blind Sight Series
See Me

Burning With Desire
Craving the Heat
Firehouse Romance Complete Collection

Forging Billions Series
Dirty Money
Petty Cash
Payment Required

For His Pleasure
Elizabeth
Georgia
Madison

Fortune Riders MC Series
Billionaire Biker
Billionaire Ransom
Billionaire Misery

Fragile Series
Fragile Touch
Fragile Kiss
Fragile Love

Great Temptation Series
The Devil's Footsteps
Heaven's Command
Mortals Surrender

Hades' Spawn Motorcycle Club
One You Can't Forget
One That Got Away
One That Came Back
One You Never Leave
One Christmas Night
Hades' Spawn MC Complete Series

Hard Rocked Series
Rhyme
Harmony
Lyrics

Heart of Stone Series
The Protector
The Guardian
The Warrior

Heart of the Battle Series

Celtic Viking
Celtic Rune
Celtic Mann
Heart of the Battle Series Box Set

Heistdom Series
Master Thief
Goldmine
Diamond Heist
Smile For Me
Your Move
Green With Envy
Saving Money

Highlander Wolf Series
Pack Run
Pack Land
Pack Rules

How To Love A Spy
The Secret
The Secret Life
The Secret Wife

Just About Series
About Love

About Truth
About Forever

Justice Series
Seeking Justice
Finding Justice
Chasing Justice
Pursuing Justice
Justice - Complete Series

Kissed by Billions
Kissed by Passion
Kissed by Desire
Kissed by Love

Leaning Towards Trouble
Trouble
Discord
Tenacity

Love You Series
Love Life
Need Love
My Love

Managing the Billionaire
Never Enough
Worth the Cost
Secret Admirers
Chasing Affection
Pressing Romance
Timeless Memories

Managing the Bosses Series
The Boss
The Boss Too
Who's the Boss Now
Love the Boss
I Do the Boss
Wife to the Boss
Employed by the Boss
Brother to the Boss
Senior Advisor to the Boss
Forever the Boss
Christmas With the Boss
Billionaire in Control
Billionaire Makes Millions
Billionaire at Work
Precious Little Thing
Priceless Love
Valentine Love
Gift for the Boss - Novella 3.5
Managing the Bosses Box Set #1-3

Neverending Dream - Part 2
Neverending Dream - Part 3
Neverending Dream - Part 4
Neverending Dream - Part 5

Outside the Octagon
Submit
Fight
Knockout

Protecting Diana Series
Her Bodyguard
Her Defender
Her Champion
Her Protector
Her Forever

Protecting Layla Series
His Mission
His Objective
His Devotion

Racing Hearts Series
Rush
Pace
Fast

Regency Romance Series
The Duchess Scandal - Part 1
The Duchess Scandal - Part 2

Reverse Harem Series
Primals
Archaic
Unitary

RIP Series
Track the Ripper
Hunt the Ripper
Pursue the Ripper

R&S Rich and Single Series
Alex Reid
Parker

Saving Forever
Saving Forever - Part 1
Saving Forever - Part 2
Saving Forever - Part 3
Saving Forever - Part 4
Saving Forever - Part 5

Spelling Love Series
The Author
The Book Boyfriend
The Words of Love

Taboo Wedding Series
He Loves Me Not
With This Ring
Happily Ever After

Tattooist Series
Confession of a Tattooist
Surrender of a Tattooist
Heart of a Tattooist
Hopes & Dreams of a Tattooist

Tennessee Romance
Whisky Lullaby
Whisky Melody
Whisky Harmony

The Bad Boy Alpha Club
Battle Lines - Part 1
Battle Lines

The Brush Of Love Series
Every Night
Every Day
Every Time
Every Way
Every Touch

The Debt
The Debt: Part 1 - Damn Horse
The Debt: Complete Collection

The Fire Inside Series
Dare Me
Defy Me
Burn Me

The Golden Mail
Hot Off the Press
Extra! Extra!
Read All About It
Stop the Press
Breaking News
This Just In

The Lucky Billionaire Series
Lucky Break
Streak of Luck
Lucky in Love

The Sound of Breaking Hearts Series
Disruption
Destroy
Devoted

The University of Gatica Series
The Recruiting Trip
Faster
Higher
Stronger
Dominate
No Rush
University of Gatica - The Complete Series

T.N.T. Series
Troubled Nate Thomas - Part 1
Troubled Nate Thomas - Part 2
Troubled Nate Thomas - Part 3

Undercover Series
Perfect For Me
Perfect For You
Perfect For Us

Unknown Identity Series
Unknown
Unpublished
Unexposed
Unsure
Unwritten
Unknown Identity Box Set: Books #1-3

Unlucky Series
Unlucky in Love
UnWanted
UnLoved Forever

War Torn Letters Series
My Sweetheart
My Darling
My Beloved

Wet & Wild Series

Stormy Love
Savage Love
Secure Love

Worth It Series
Worth Billions
Worth Every Cent
Worth More Than Money

You & Me - A Bad Boy Romance
Just Me
Touch Me
Kiss Me

Standalone
Wash
Loving Charity
Summer Lovin'
Love & College
Billionaire Heart
First Love
Frisky and Fun Romance Box Collection
Beating Hades' Bikers

Watch for more at www.lexytimms.com.

BLIND SIGHT SERIES

SEE Me

USA TODAY BESTSELLING AUTHOR

LEXY TIMMS

Copyright 2020

Blind Sight Series

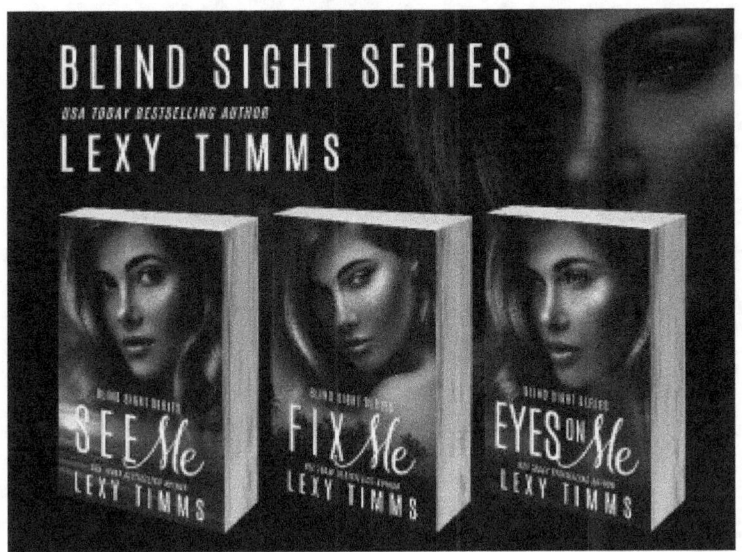

Book 1 – See Me

Book 2 – Fix Me

Book 3 – Eyes on Me

Find Lexy Timms:

LEXY TIMMS NEWSLETTER:
http://eepurl.com/9i0vD
Lexy Timms Facebook Page:
https://www.facebook.com/SavingForever
Lexy Timms Website:
http://www.lexytimms.com

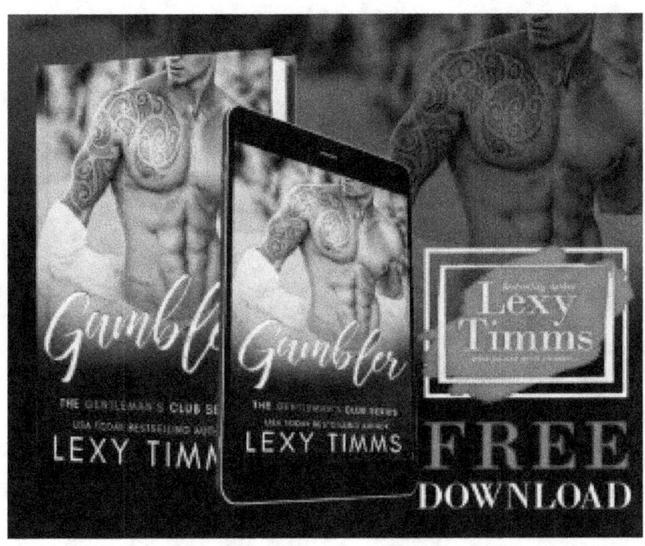
Gambler
Gambler
THE GENTLEMAN'S CLUB SERIES
USA TODAY BESTSELLING AUTHOR
LEXY TIMMS
Lexy Timms
FREE
DOWNLOAD

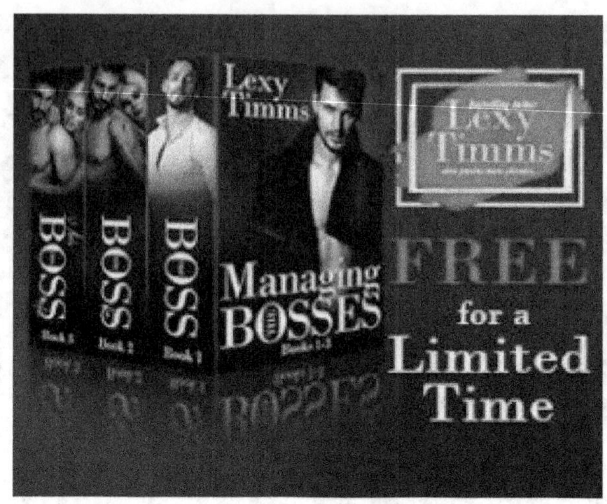

Want to read more...
For **FREE?**
Sign up for Lexy Timms' newsletter
And she'll send you updates on new releases, ARC copies of books
and a whole lotta fun!
Sign up for news and updates!
http://eepurl.com/9i0vD

See Me Blurb:

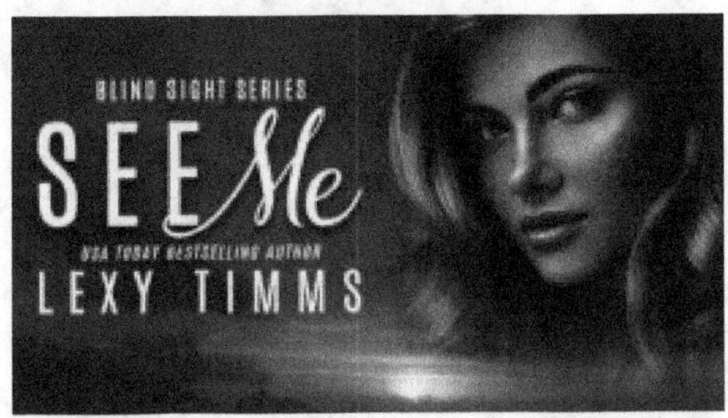

"SOMETIMES THE HEART sees what is invisible to the eye."

Bree was the type of woman who relished in the joy of her existence. She was always outside, she surfed, painted and helped out at local charities. She had a ton of friends and she was in a serious relationship.

Until her life came to an abrupt halt. After a bad breakup, she was in a car accident and she lost her sight through blunt force trauma to her face. She should have counted her blessings, she knew that. She could have lost her life.

But suddenly, everything is drenched in black. She knows the beauty of the world is out there, but she can't reach it. And she hates her life, now. No matter how hard her friends and her father are trying to help her live again.

When her father hires a caregiver to look after her, Bree's furious. She needs her sight back, not a babysitter.

And damned if she's not going to spend every minute resenting it all and hating her life.

Chapter One

Bree

"Dammit!" I shouted, jumping up from the couch and dropping the remote in the process. "Why do you always have to do this?"

"Bree, you're being ridiculous!" Nate shouted back. "What're you ticked about now? You're always friggin' pissed."

I closed my eyes, shaking my head. "I'm not always pissed. I'm tired of you constantly asking me when we're going to get married. We can't even agree on what kind of takeout we want. How do you think we're ready to get married?"

He stepped towards me, trying to take my hands. I pulled away, moving around the coffee table. He looked at me, his dark eyes flashing with irritation. For a brief moment, I remembered how handsome I used to think he was. I suppose he still was handsome, but to me, he was mostly just annoying now. To me, he'd become like a scratchy wool blanket, wrapped around me and irritating me like crazy.

"Bree, it's a stupid fight over pizza or Chinese. Married couples fight over things like that. We're normal. You're making a mountain out of a molehill. As usual."

"Nate, we're not married," I said, scoffing at his attitude. "It isn't just about the fact that I wanted Chinese. It's everything. Every. Little. Thing."

He shook his head, putting his hands on his hips as he stared at me with an expression that reminded me so much of my father. I felt like I was being scolded. Was he going to ground me because I didn't want to go to the stupid bridal fair? "You're throwing a fit because you want to go out with your friends instead of planning our wedding. That's what this is about. You're picking a fight and hoping I'll just give up."

Growling with frustration, I felt an unreasonable urge to stomp my foot. "I'm not going to eat cake with you! I don't give a shit what kind of cake there is! Why do we have to eat cake this weekend anyway?"

Feeling on the edge of hysterical, I was aware I was overreacting, but it had been building for a good year. The whole subject was a constant source of irritation for me. He was always bugging me about doing this or that for our wedding. The final straw had been the fight over him insisting we have pizza and watch a stupid Rom-com.

"We've been dating for three years, engaged for two. When are we ever going to make this happen? I'm tired of waiting. I want to get married and start a family."

Blowing out a breath, I tried to calm myself down. "I told you when you asked me to marry you that I wasn't ready. You said you were okay with taking it slow."

"That was two years ago."

"Yeah, and it feels like every day since you've asked me when we're going to get married. You don't think I've noticed the magazines or the random emails I get, or the tickets to the bridal fair? You're pressuring me and I don't like it."

He came around trying to touch me again. "Okay, I'll back off. I'm sorry. I thought you just needed a little push."

I threw my arms up. "A little push! You are about as subtle as a bull in a china shop!"

"Stop it!" he shouted. "You're just acting like a child. Three fucking years, Bree. How long are you going to string me along?"

I narrowed my eyes at him. "I'm not stringing you along. Why are you in such a fucking hurry to get married? I'm twenty-five, you're twenty-six. We're not exactly pushing up against old age. I want to live.

I want to be free. I don't want to be a wife. I liked what we had before, but lately, you've become so serious, so pushy. So damn bossy!"

"I'm supposed to be your fiancé, your future husband. I'm not being bossy. I care about you and want to ensure you make good decisions. I'm trying to help you be the best you can be. You flit around doing nothing with your life."

I laughed. "You are not my father. I'm a grown woman. I don't need your guidance. You need to worry about yourself. And I certainly don't 'flit around,' as you said," unable to keep the sarcasm from her voice. "I spent four years in college, working my ass off, and now I am trying to get my gallery off the ground. I have a lot going on right now, and a wedding is the last thing I want to think about. You need to back off."

"I can't do that. I love you and you're going to be my wife. We need to start thinking about our future. We need to save our money and think about buying our own house. Your dad said he would help us out. You don't even need to work. He'll support you."

"I don't want to live off his money! I want to be independent!"

He made a disgusted sound. "You don't have to pretend with me. You were born rich. You'll always be rich. You've played at being Little Miss Independent long enough. It's time to settle down and live the life you were born into."

"Wow." I stared at him and in that moment, realized he was not the man I thought I loved. He was not a man I could spend the rest of my life with. Somewhere, in the back of my mind, I had known he wasn't the one. I had hoped he eventually would be, but it wasn't getting any better. His family had money, but nothing like my father. Listening to him talk this way gave me the feeling my appeal to him was more about my trust fund than the person I was.

"Nate, I can't do this anymore," I said, with total exhaustion. I couldn't pretend. I didn't have the strength or even the desire to pretend we would be okay.

"Let's sit down. We can watch that survival show if you want. You're tired. I'm tired. We'll sleep on it and tomorrow we'll go to that little café on the beach you like so much."

He was trying to appease me now. This was how most of our fights went. We got mad, he insisted we leave it alone and never talk about what was really going on. Burying our problems all this time had resulted in the mountain he insisted I was making.

"It's not about watching what I want," I told him. "I'm tired of always fighting. We fight over every little thing. Aren't you tired of it? We can't spend ten minutes together without arguing about something stupid."

He waved a hand. "We'll work through it. Growing pains, you know. We have to learn how to live with each other. All couples go through this."

"Well, it's not for me. I don't want to get used to it or work through it. I'm done."

He flinched, glaring at me. "You don't get to say we're done."

My eyebrows shot up. "Excuse me? I think I can."

He shook his head. "No, you don't. I did not hang on for three fucking years, putting up with your spoiled princess bullshit for you to dump me before we get down the aisle. This is just another one of your tantrums. You'll get over it."

My mouth fell open. "Spoiled princess? I am no such thing."

"You are daddy's little girl. You know you have him wrapped around your little finger. You're just pissed because I don't bow down to you."

"I'm out of here," I hissed snatching my purse and keys off the table.

"Bree, wait!" he shouted.

I didn't stop. I slammed the door and walked as fast as my legs would carry me to my car. He had crossed a line. I was so glad I'd been able to see his true colors before I actually married his sorry ass.

Slamming the car door, I started the BMW and hit the gas. I was spoiled, but that didn't mean I was a brat. I couldn't help that my father was wealthy. He liked to buy me things. It wasn't like I asked for it. It made my dad happy to take care of me. He deserved to have some happiness in his life.

I jumped on the Pacific Highway, wanting to feel the wind in my hair. I rolled down the window and blasted the radio. I didn't care that it was raining. I leaned my face closer to the window and let the rain splash against me before I realized my leather seats were getting soaked. I pushed the button, rolling up the window and putting the wipers on high. I replayed the argument in my head, slapping my hand against the steering wheel. I was so pissed.

How dare he speak to me like a child! His overdone caring and doting ways had gotten old fast. He smothered me. He tried to stop me from doing the things I liked, cautioning me against the dangers of everything under the sun. I screamed out loud, slapping my hand against the steering wheel again. I hated being coddled.

I was furious that I had wasted three years of my life with him. Three years! I could have dated and gone out with my friends more. I could have gone on that ski trip instead of letting him talk me out of it. I felt like I had missed out on so much because I had let him dictate what I should and shouldn't do. No more.

That's it. I was going to start living my life the way I wanted to. I had waited too long to truly live. I was going to surf more often. Paint more. Live more. Just be me. I had lost myself at some point in this relationship and had shriveled up a little more each day.

"No more!" I shouted, cranking the stereo higher.

Glancing down at the speedometer, I realized I was speeding, but I didn't care. The highway was mine that night. I needed to put distance between Nate and myself. I was going back to Malibu and tomorrow morning, first thing, I was going for a run on the beach. Then I was going to go by new art supplies and start painting again.

My phone rang. I looked around, wondering where I had put it. It was sitting on the passenger seat. Nate's face was on the screen. I shook my head and put my eyes back on the road. I was not interested in what he had to say.

Headlights were coming my way, so I let off the gas a bit, just in case it was a cop. I noticed the headlights were that of a semi-truck. The lights shone bright in my eyes. I looked away, nearly blinded by the glare coming off the rain-soaked street.

The headlights jerked into my lane, startling me. Both hands went to the steering wheel. The lights swerved back into the left lane. Everything happened fast. The lights flashed again before the cab of the truck whipped to the side. Then, out of nowhere, the trailer slid out, coming directly at me.

Immediately hitting the brakes, I screamed, but the wet pavement was slick. My BMW spun to the right, so I was sideways across the road and sliding for the trailer. There was nothing I could do. The impact slammed against the passenger side of my car. My head hit the window a split second before the airbag deployed. I heard tires squealing and metal crunching as my car bounced around, violently slamming into one hard object after another.

At some point, I became aware that the screaming was coming from me. The car came to a rest and then there was nothing but silence. I blinked, trying to take a mental inventory of my injuries. I couldn't see anything. I closed my eyes. Everything felt wrong.

My head was a mess. I couldn't seem to hold a thought and the need to rest was powerful. I knew I should call the police. I needed help. Unfortunately, my hands wouldn't move. Nothing moved. Darkness pulled at me. I wanted to stay awake and call for help. I couldn't.

Unsure of how much time had passed, I could hear sirens in the distance, barely audible over the rain pounding on the roof of my car. I still couldn't see anything. It had been a dark night. With no headlights, it was pitch black.

I tried to stay awake. I wanted to tell the paramedics my leg hurt. And my head. My head really hurt. The sirens grew louder as the darkness took hold. I faded into the blissful black sea that freed me from the pain gripping my body.

Chapter Two

Luke

IT WAS NEVER TOO LATE to start over. At least, that's what I was going to keep telling myself. I was twenty-eight and leaving home for the first time. I guess you could say I was a late bloomer. It wasn't so much about blooming late, but more about being a mama's boy. Not in the sense that I needed my mother, but the other way around.

She needed me. She depended on me. It wasn't until after talking to one of my buddies from the psych ward at the hospital where I worked, that I realized I was in a very unhealthy relationship with my mother. Not in a creepy Bates way. A different kind of unhealthy. An unhealthy that a lot of other people were in and didn't even realize it. It was a codependent relationship.

I don't know why I didn't see it. I was an RN after all. But the relationship was toxic. The life was being sucked from my veins and the only way I could save myself was to run away. I was running away, and I wasn't afraid to admit it. I didn't give a shit what people thought about me leaving the way I was. They weren't the ones walking in my shoes. I couldn't keep doing what everyone else thought I was supposed to do.

I was getting the hell out of Dallas and I wasn't looking back. Like so many other young people, young being a flexible word, I was heading out to sunny California with the hopes of starting over and fulfilling my dreams. I had stars in my eyes. I didn't want to be famous or rich, but I wanted to be free.

The sun and the beaches were what I wanted. I was over the damn hurricanes. I wanted to be a beach bum. I may have been a little late to the party to sow my wild oats, but there was no time like the present. Los Angeles meant freedom. Freedom from my mother and all the drama that was back in Dallas. I had loved my job at the hospital, but I couldn't keep living the life I was in. The life I had carved out in Dallas had become me doing everything for my mom. I had little time or freedom to do anything I wanted to do—including dating.

I had a glimpse into my future one night while treating a patient in the emergency department and realized I was destined to be the fifty-year-old bachelor taking care of his abusive mother if I didn't get out now. I didn't want to be that miserable guy barely hanging on to his sanity. I didn't want to give up my chance of finding a wife and raising my own family because I was too busy taking care of my mother. She'd had her chance at life. She had been married and got to have children. Now it was my turn.

With my RN license and a good work record, I was confident that with the nursing shortages all over the country, I would land a job fairly quickly. I could do in-home care, work in a clinic, or even in a hospital. I was flexible and had the experience in all fields to broaden my horizons. I knew the cost of living was brutal, but I was hoping to use my savings to make up for the cut in pay until I found something good. I could eat ramen noodles if I had to. I was willing to sacrifice just about anything to make my life in California work.

If all else failed, I figured I could get some modeling jobs if I had to. Although in LA, everyone was likely to be an aspiring model or an actor. The competition would be stiffer, and I was a little past my expiration date in the modeling world, but I would do hemorrhoid ads if I had to. Hell, I would even do the STD prevention ads if that's what it took to stay in LA.

Modeling had paid my way through college and my agent did occasionally call and ask if I wanted to pick up some work here and there.

The jobs were there if I chose to go after them. I had stopped modeling when I started working fulltime as a nurse. Modeling had been fun, but it had never been my dream job. I had a portfolio and experience, which gave me a slight advantage. Slight. Very slight.

I was going to stay positive. I had to focus on the good. If nursing didn't work and modeling failed, I would be a damn barista. I would dress up in a furry animal costume and hold up a sign on a street corner. I had to try everything. I couldn't go back to Dallas with my tail between my legs and admit defeat. That would certainly give my mother a great deal of satisfaction. I couldn't do it. I refused to do it.

"You won't quit," I murmured, glancing up to look at myself in the rearview mirror. "You won't give up. You will live in your damn car if you have to. Dallas is not an option."

Focusing on the long stretch of road in front of me, I settled in. I had everything I needed stuffed into the back of my Nissan Maxima. I had sold all my furniture, including my precious big screen TV, deciding it made sense to drive out rather than rent a U-Haul.

I had found a semi-furnished apartment in LA. It wasn't great, but from the pictures I saw, it would be okay until I could find something better. There was no lease, which made it appealing. Part of me was hesitant to lock myself into a contract. If things didn't work out in LA, I told myself I could always head north until I found somewhere to land. Anything was better than going back home and conceding defeat.

My phone rang and I didn't have to guess who it was. It was her. She'd been calling almost every hour on the hour since I had left. Hell, before I had even gotten out of the apartment. I looked at the screen and saw it was my mom. I had been dodging her calls, but she wasn't going to stop. If I didn't talk to her now, she would only keep calling. Plus, there was that little niggling sense of responsibility telling me I had to answer. There was always a chance something was actually wrong. A slim chance, but a chance, nonetheless.

I pushed the button to answer the call on my Bluetooth speaker system. "Hello, Mom."

"Luke!" she exclaimed. "I've been calling," she whined. "Why didn't you answer?"

"I've been driving, Mom. I didn't have service for a while."

"This is silly. Come home. I don't know why you're doing this."

It was the same conversation. "Because I want a fresh start. We've talked about this many times over the last month."

"You don't need a fresh start," she snapped. "You have a life here in Dallas. You have a good job and a mother who needs you. You aren't a wild, young man. You're almost thirty."

"I don't have a job anymore. I quit, remember? I quit because I'm moving to California. I hired a caregiver for you. Someone will check on you once a week."

"Luke, that's not good enough. I need you to take care of me. Only you know what I like. Those caregivers rob you blind. They take advantage of the elderly and infirm."

I sighed. "You are not elderly, and you are not infirm. I'm a caregiver. I don't steal from anyone. You said you needed some help. I got you some help."

"It isn't the same," she said, her voice filled with emotion.

Briefly, I closed my eyes. I knew she was crying. She always cried when she didn't get her way. "Mom, I need to do this. Will you please support me in this?"

"I have been sick all day. I need your help."

"I'm sorry, but if you aren't feeling well, get some rest. I went grocery shopping for you before I left. You have plenty of your favorite foods. Heat up some soup and watch one of your shows. You'll feel better in no time."

"Why are you doing this to me?" she wailed. "You're all I have and you're leaving me."

She sounded pitiful. It went against every grain of my being to ignore her pleas. I was the kind of person that felt other people's pain and suffering right down to my very core. I had been called an empath on more than one occasion. It was why I chose to be a nurse instead of a doctor. I wanted more of the hands-on care. I wanted to be the one comforting someone on the worst day of their life. I wanted to nurse people back to health.

To ignore her calls for help was killing me a little, but I had to do it. "Mom, I love you, but I know you are going to be okay. It's time for me to live my own life. I've taken care of you for a very long time. I need to do this for myself. I hired you someone to check in on you. If you don't like that, then you can look for someone else. I can't do it. I have to do this for myself."

I heard her sniffling and knew she was crying in earnest. "I can't believe my own son is abandoning me. Everyone always leaves me."

"I'll call you when I get to LA. Goodbye."

I ended the call before she could say anything else. It would only be more of the same. My hands shook as I held the wheel. It took a lot for me to shut her down. I had been programmed my whole life to take care of her. If she cried, I wiped her tears—and there were a lot of tears shed over the last twenty-eight years.

Wiping a hand over my face, I tried to shed the heavy feeling of guilt that was clinging to me. I had to shake it off. I was doing the right thing and had told myself those same words at least a million times. I had to live my life. I had already wasted enough time. Life was short. I saw that first-hand every day I went to work. Death wasn't picky. I didn't want to be the guy that was riding his bike home from work and got hit by a truck in a freak accident. I didn't want to die before I had a chance to live.

Sure, I was probably being dramatic, but a few months back a feeling had taken hold inside me that I just couldn't shake. I woke up one day and realized I wasn't happy. I wasn't fulfilled. I needed more.

My mother was an energy drain, literally sucking the life out of me. Whether it was intentional or not, she was.

For a long time, I had resented my father for walking out and leaving me and my sister behind, but I was beginning to understand why he left.

Chapter Three

Bree

"UP ONE STEP," MY FATHER coached, his hand on my elbow as he guided me through the front door of the mansion I had grown up in.

I used my foot to find the step and walked inside. The natural reaction to turn on the lights was still something I was struggling with. A month in rehab hadn't done a lot of good. I still wanted to turn on the lights. I wanted to see. I was sick of the blackness that had swallowed me whole and refused to release me.

"Where's the stairs?" I asked, feeling a little disorientated.

"I've given you one of the bedrooms downstairs," he answered. "It doesn't make sense for you to go up and down those stairs. It's too risky."

It was yet another in a long series of blows. "Fine," I mumbled. I didn't have the strength to care. I was all cared out. I had cried and raged until I was exhausted and nothing changed the facts. I was blind. My life as I had known it was over and I would never be able to do the things I loved.

"About ten more feet," he said, keeping his voice gentle.

I was sick of being handled with kid gloves. I was sick of being blind. I was sick of being trapped. I walked through the door of what had once been a guest suite. I knew it had a big bathroom and a bank of windows that faced the gardens in the courtyard. The backyard was beautiful. It was private and secluded and I had always felt like I had my own personal park right out the back door.

Fat lot of good it did now. I couldn't see the roses or the lilies I loved so much. I couldn't see the pretty fountain that lit up with a rainbow of colors every night. I was probably not going to be allowed in the backyard by myself, assuming I could even find my way.

"Here we are," he said, infusing his voice with fake cheer.

"Yeah, my new cell."

"I've had fresh bedding put on. We have an intercom system as well. All you need to do is speak out. It's like Alexa on steroids. She can play anything you want, call anyone you want, send texts—everything."

"Great, thanks."

"Your bed is directly in front of you, about ten steps," he said, using the tips the rehab people had given him. That would be my life now. Darkness and counting steps.

"Thanks." I reached out, taking small steps until I felt the bed against my legs.

"Can I get you something to drink?" he offered.

"No."

"Are you hungry? I had Nellie pick up your favorite foods. We have all the dishes the therapist recommended as well. You're all set. We'll make you as comfortable as you can while you adjust to your new life."

"I'm never going to adjust," I snapped. "I don't want to adjust. Buying every bit of technology for blind people isn't going to help me adjust."

"Actually, I think it will. We want to do everything we can to give you as much independence as possible. With time, you'll be more comfortable with the situation. The assistive technologies will give you your life back."

I turned around, not knowing exactly where he was but attempting to look in his general idea. "I'm twenty-five and moving back home. That's not exactly independent. I'll never get my life back. I'm blind,

Dad. I'm officially disabled and dependent on someone to take care of me."

"We've talked about you moving into your own place once you've had time to—"

"Time to accept that I'm blind?" I asked. "Time to accept I'm going to be an invalid for the rest of my life? Time to learn how to cook for myself when I can't see? Or clean up? Wash my clothes? Do you know how different our worlds are now? I can't watch TV or go to a movie or watch people surf! I'm stuck in this black box with no way out!"

"You're not an invalid. There are plenty of visually impaired people that live independent lives. They have jobs, live on their own and have families. You will learn a new normal, but that's getting way ahead of the game. We don't know if this is permanent."

"Yes, we do know. Don't try and give me false hope. The doctors have already made it clear."

"I'm not giving up," he said. "There are hundreds of specialists and I have reached out to all of them."

"Don't dad," I said with exhaustion. "Just stop. It doesn't do either of us any good."

"You're not a quitter. I'm not a quitter. I won't stop until every avenue has been exhausted."

"I'm tired," I told him. My dad exhausted me. He was absolutely certain he was fighting some invisible enemy and wasn't going to give up until he won. I had given up weeks ago.

"Gabrielle," he started. Anytime he used my full name it meant a lecture was forthcoming.

"What? I'm tired, Dad."

"Don't give up," he said.

"I'm tired," I said again.

I couldn't listen to another pep talk. I was exhausted, physically and emotionally. I knew he thought it was helpful. It wasn't. Not anymore. I had been told no too many times.

"Alright, I'll check back in on you later."

I groaned. "You don't have to check on me, Dad. I'm a big girl."

"Do you need anything before I leave?" he asked.

"No."

I heard his footsteps walking away and then the click of the door softly closing. I sighed with relief and sat down on the bed. I kicked off my flats and stretched out on the bed. It seemed silly to close my eyes when I was already submerged in darkness, but I did it anyway.

Birds. I could hear birds just beyond the window. I didn't remember ever hearing birds before when I lived at the mansion. The therapist I had worked with at the rehab center told me that my other senses would be heightened. He had told me to tune into my hearing and my sense of smell. Some of it seemed enhanced but I wasn't going to be catching any flies with chopsticks anytime soon.

Back at the rehab center, I had been put into an art class. I thought it was ridiculous, but they insisted I could still do what I loved. I was certain they were full of shit and I was sick of everyone trying to tell me being blind wasn't a big deal. It was a huge deal to me. I was coping, but I wasn't living.

I was tired of being tired. The headaches I still suffered from were becoming fewer and farther between, but they were still there. My head was pounding. The doctors told me my recovery would take months, possibly years. They told me I would never be the person I was before that truck driver lost control and slammed into my car. Everyone kept telling me I was lucky to be alive, lucky the worst lasting injury I'd suffered was losing my sight.

For weeks following the accident, I had been in a coma. My poor father had been put through the ringer, thinking he would lose me. I was thankful to be alive, but there were moments when I struggled to be happy about it. When I first woke up, I didn't understand why it was so dark, and I'd had a panic attack when they told me I had lost my sight.

Even now, I struggled with it. I wasn't necessarily afraid of the dark, but all I saw was dark. I had been medicated for weeks to keep me from having panic attacks. I still had the bottle of meds for when it happened again. My doctors had tried to give me coping methods, but sometimes I felt as if I was in a tiny, windowless box.

I felt a tear slide down my cheek, and I rubbed it away. That was one of the perks of being blind. I couldn't put on makeup. When I cried, I didn't have to worry about raccoon eyes. I tried to imagine what I looked like. I didn't think I was a vain person, but I did like putting on makeup. I liked to dress up. I liked to look nice. Now, I didn't even know if I was putting on matching shoes half the time.

Still, I didn't want to be a crybaby. I wasn't a crybaby. I was a strong, independent woman. Scratch the independent part. I was still strong. Kind of. Another tear slid down my face. A counselor told me it was normal to grieve, since I had suffered a loss.

I had lost my sight, which was a huge part of me. And I was grieving the loss of the woman I was. The woman I would never be again. Surfing, painting, shopping and going out to clubs—it was gone. A sob escaped my lips. I tried not to cry in front of my dad. I knew he was grieving too, but trying to be strong for me. So I only cried when I was alone.

After crying it out for a solid thirty minutes, I was left feeling emotionally drained. My cell phone rang. That was something else I hated. I now had stupid ringtones for all my main contacts. The phone had been programmed to announce the caller, which was super embarrassing. I had demanded one of the nurses take off the stupid voice thing and put on the specialized ringers instead.

In this case, I didn't recognize the ring, and decided it wasn't worth me answering. They could leave a voicemail if they felt like they needed to talk to me. It was probably just one of the many therapists I was working with. I had a physical therapist to help me get back into good physical shape after being in the coma. I had a rehab specialist team that helped me with all kinds of things, like learning to eat without seeing and even using the bathroom.

Then there was my shrink. My dad had hired a small army to help me. It was how he handled things. He threw money at anything that wasn't going his way. My being blind was not going his way, and I couldn't help but think that he would be better off without me. I was a now officially a burden. I knew he would be sad if I was gone but he would move on.

If I was a constant burden right under his nose, it was only going to wear him down. It would wear both of us down. What kind of future would I have? Was I supposed to live in his house for the rest of my days? Was he supposed to take care of me for the rest of his life? My dad would give up anything for me. I knew that, but I didn't want him doing that. He deserved happiness. My being around his place would only lead to more misery.

Rolling to my side, I curled up in a ball and cried myself to sleep. I found myself preferring to live in a dream world. When I dreamed, I could see. But it was always old memories. Memories of me and Nate. Memories of me surfing. Unfortunately, the dreams were hard to find in the sea of nightmares that always found their way into my dark world. The accident seemed to be on a loop, constant replaying in my head until I woke up crying out.

I had pills for that as well. Pills that knocked me out and blocked out all the dreams and nightmares. Then there were pills that took away the pain. Pills that were supposed to help my optic nerve or some shit. Pills, pills and more pills. My life was reduced to knowing the time and when to take what pills.

I couldn't do it. I could spend the rest of my days here with no hope for a future. With no happiness. No excitement. No love. No sex. Obviously, I could have sex without seeing, but how was I going to meet a man? How would I know if I was banging an old guy or a troll? There were too many variables. I had decided some time ago that I would be spending the rest of my days single and celibate.

Chapter Four

Luke

MY APARTMENT WAS NOT in the best part of town. That was the problem with renting or buying sight unseen without knowing the city. Realtors and rental agents didn't advertise their rental was on the next block over from a known gang hangout. They didn't tell you prostitutes and their pimps roamed the parking lot at night.

Unfortunately, there wasn't a lot I could do just yet about my living situation. I couldn't find a damn job. A couple of the hospitals I had applied to were under hiring freezes. I had put in my application to numerous clinics, even the free ones, and had heard nothing. I had gotten a couple interviews, but it was always the same line of bullshit about they'll call if they'd like to hire me.

I was qualified, and I had excellent references. I knew what the issue was. I was young and I was a man. Despite how normal that was, some people still had a real thing about young guys being a nurse. They either assumed I was gay or a pervert.

Staring out the window of my tiny apartment, I watched what appeared to be a drug deal and shook my head. I had to get out of my current living situation. I had enough savings left to pick up and either head down to San Diego or go up north to San Francisco.

I had only been in LA for a few days, but I was already starting to get discouraged. I had fooled myself into thinking it would be relatively easy. The bigger the city, the more jobs available. I didn't take into consideration there would be a lot more people fighting for those same jobs. Nurses with twenty years of experience versus my five years.

At the moment, it felt as though I may have made one of the worst decisions of my life. I had a good job and a place to live back home, but I had given it all up to chase a dream. My mom was right. I was too old to be making childish mistakes like that. I should have known better. I should have secured a job before I quit my other one.

"Smooth move, Luke. Smooth move," I muttered.

Bored and tired of spending all my time in the tiny apartment, I decided to go out. I had come to LA for the sun and I had yet to enjoy the excitement of living in the city. I could afford a couple beers. I was hoping to meet some people and start to settle in. Maybe they would have some connections.

Then again, I wasn't sure a bar was the best place to pick up connections to work in the medical field. Although, back in Dallas, there was a bar near the hospital where all the doctors and nurses hung out after their shifts. Maybe I could find the hang out and get a lead on some job openings.

I walked into the small bedroom with the twin bed that had not been mentioned in the ad for the furnished apartment. I was six-two. The bed was not meant for a man my size. My feet hung off the end. It was a problem I was hoping to remedy soon, but if I didn't get a job, I couldn't buy a bed.

Refusing to give up, I was determined not to focus on the negative. Difficult times were part of life. I would push through and come out on the other side stronger for it. A few beers or maybe something a little stronger would help the difficult times to feel less difficult. At least I hoped so.

My phone started to ring. I felt my pockets, realized I was in my underwear and quickly scanned the bedroom. This could be a job interview! I raced back into the living space and saw it sitting on the couch. I dove for it, praying like hell my luck was about to change.

"Shit," I groaned, seeing my mom's phone number on the screen.

I couldn't talk to her just then. She would only start whining and begging me to go back home. She would put on one hell of a guilt trip that would compound the regret I was already feeling. I hit the decline button and let it go to voicemail. She had been calling every single day. Ten times at least. The woman was relentless. She said she was sick, but with the energy she was using simply to bug the hell out of me, I knew otherwise.

She would have to wait. I needed to get my head on straight before I could deal with her drama. I didn't want her to find my weak spot and pick at it until I caved in and gave up. I didn't want to quit. I wouldn't let her bully me into tucking my tail between my legs and heading home.

I changed into a clean button-up shirt and khaki shorts. I wanted to fit in with the crowd and the shorts and shirt thing seemed to be the general style here. I liked the laid-back nature of things and was going to take full advantage of it while I could.

Walking down the street, I headed for the part of town I knew to be a little better than my own neighborhood at the moment. The weather was warm, but not too hot and there was very little humidity. It felt good. The air was a little smoggy and polluted with who knew what I was breathing in, but I was in LA and that was awesome.

I found a bar that looked to be fairly decent. I didn't see any riffraff hanging around the front door and decided it was safe to go in. I looked around, surveying the scene. It was a typical sports bar with TVs mounted on the walls, pool tables in back and the usual bar setup with pictures of the local teams. I wasn't a Rams fan and never would be, but I'd keep that to myself.

The place was relatively empty. A few guys were at a table laughing and enjoying their beers. I pegged them for blue-collar workers. There were a few more guys at the pool table, one of them wearing a tiny blond woman who seemed to have it in her head she was his coat or something. She was completely wrapped around him.

All in all, it looked like a peaceful bar, a place a man could get a drink and relax without fear of finding himself in a bar fight. I hated the rough honky-tonks back home. That was something else that was missing—sawdust and boots. I realized the floor was polished to a high shine and there wasn't a single blade of grass, straw or horseshit. A definite bonus. Although I kind of missed the smell of cow shit and alfalfa sometimes.

I sauntered up to the bar, checking out the pretty little thing with her beautiful backside to me. "Hello," I said to grab her attention.

She turned around, looked me up and down. "Let me guess, a beer."

I grinned. "I would love a beer."

"Light, I suppose."

Slowly, I shook my head. "Hell no."

That finally pulled a smile from her. "Coming right up." She handed me the beer. "Visiting?" she asked.

"Just moved here, actually."

Her smile slipped. "Let me guess, you're an aspiring actor?"

I laughed. "Nope. I'm a nurse."

"You drive a hearse?"

I rolled my eyes. "That's about right."

She grinned again. "Really? Are you an actual nurse or you're hoping to play one on TV?"

"I'm an actual nurse. I just moved here from Dallas and I'm looking for a fresh start."

"I thought I detected a bit of a twang. Dallas huh? Did you grow up on a cattle ranch? Are you wearing cowboy boots?"

"No boots and no ranch. Dallas isn't exactly a small town with cows roaming the streets."

There was a commotion behind me. The bartender got a look of disgust on her face as three men walked in. One was obviously very drunk. His two buddies were trying to hold him up and steer him towards a table.

"Great," she muttered.

"Is it normal to be that drunk at five o'clock around here?"

She let out a long sigh. "Normal for some," she answered, before sliding down the bar to take the drink orders.

Taking a drink from my beer, I was trying to ignore the ruckus coming from the table. I did my best to ignore it, focusing on the golf tournament on the TV above the bar. I had no interest in golf, but I was trying to play it cool. The one guy was cursing and going on about some woman that had dumped him. I couldn't imagine why she wouldn't want to be with such a standup guy.

I was halfway done with my beer when I was hit hard from behind. I spun around on the barstool and found myself face to face with the drunken idiot.

"What the hell?" I growled.

The guy sneered at me. "Yeah, what the hell? You got a problem man?"

"You bumped into me," I pointed out, not backing down from what was clearly destined to be a shoving match.

"You want to start something?" the drunk slurred.

"I'm not starting shit, but you better believe I will finish it."

His buddies rushed to his side. One of them pulled his friend back and another got in my face. "Get the fuck out of here," he snarled at me.

"Fuck you. I'm sitting here drinking a beer and minding my own business. Take your drunk ass friend home."

The guy's green eyes flashed. "Do you know who you're talking to?"

I smirked. "Nope, and I don't give a shit who you are or who your sloppy-drunk buddy is. Why don't you all go home and sleep it off."

He shoved me in the chest. The guy was my height, but I knew I outweighed him. I was a Texas boy and I could hang with the best of them. It wouldn't be my first bar fight. I could throw down, despite my pretty boy looks.

The guy sized me up and down. "You're not from here."

"Nope. Doesn't mean I can't kick your ass."

He chuckled. "Get the fuck out of here."

"Fuck you," I shot back, not the least bit intimidated.

"Austin, let's go," his buddy said. "We need to get him home."

Glaring at the guy I now knew to be named Austin, I waited for him to make his decision. I would let him hit me first, but then it was on. I would not be pushed around by anyone.

"Well?" I asked, knowing it was probably stupid to encourage him into hitting me.

"You're not worth it," he snapped and walked away.

Deep inside, I let out a sigh of relief. I was glad it didn't end up in a knock down drag out fight. I really didn't want to be sporting a black eye if I got an interview. I was supposed to be healing people, not breaking their faces, which I would have done.

Turning around, I sat back down on my stool. The bartender sauntered over and shook her head. "Not exactly the best way to make friends in a new place."

I shrugged. "I didn't start it. I'm not going to get pushed around."

"Is that because you think you have to prove yourself, and make up for the fact that you're a nurse?"

"I don't have to prove myself to anyone. I'm no less of a man because I choose to be a nurse. Only ignorant people think that. I'm certainly not a pussy."

She smiled. "Did I hit a nerve?"

"Not at all," I said, in no mood for her thinly veiled insults.

Throwing a ten-dollar bill on the bar, I walked out. I was beginning to think I might have made a mistake in choosing to move to LA. I thought I was getting a fresh start, but it didn't seem to be working out that way. I slowly walked back to my apartment, wondering if I was destined to spend the rest of my days taking care of my mother and never really having a life of my own.

Chapter Five

Bree

I WAS LISTENING TO an audiobook and facing the window. With some patience, I had managed to get the window open and could now feel a cool breeze coming through. It wasn't exactly like being on a beach or riding my bike along a quiet trail, but it was as close as I could get to being in the great outdoors. The audiobook was still droning on about something. I had lost interest about three minutes in, but I needed the background noise. I needed to pretend I was somewhere else. Someone else.

There was a soft knock on my door, but I pretended not to hear it. It was obviously my dad. He had been hounding me since I'd been forced to move in. I just wanted to be alone but he didn't seem to get it. He was smothering me with his good intentions and choking what little life I had left right out of me.

"Bree," he whispered softly through the door. "Are you asleep?"

I didn't answer, hoping he would think I was asleep and go away. He didn't. I heard the door opening, the bottom sliding over the thick carpeting in the room. It wasn't a sound I had ever heard before I was blind. I suppose it was evidence of those other senses kicking up a bit.

"Dad," I groaned. "I just want to be alone."

"You've been alone. It isn't healthy for you to sit in this room day in and day out. You need to get out. Go outside. I'll take you."

"No."

"Bree it's a beautiful day out there. You can go for a swim. Your physical therapist said it would be good for you to get in the water."

"I'll ram my face into the edge of the pool."

He softly chuckled. "You can feel the edges. You swim with your eyes closed anyway, right?"

He had a point, but I wasn't going to admit it. "I don't want to go swimming."

"Would you like to go for a walk around the grounds?"

"No, Dad. I don't want to do anything. There is no point."

"There is every point. You need to get up and get moving. Get some fresh air."

"I'm sitting in front of the open window."

He let out a loud sigh. I could hear him walking towards me and I stiffened, not wanting to be touched. His hand settled on my shoulder. I jerked away.

"You're going to waste away," he whispered. "I know you're hurting, but sulking isn't helping. You need to embrace life."

"I don't have a life. I can't live like this." I felt the sob welling up and quickly fought it back down.

"I know you're struggling and I'm part of the reason you're struggling. You've always been independent and having me try to take care of you isn't working. I get it. We need to maintain our relationship as father and daughter. I'm hiring you a caregiver to help you during the day."

"No!" I exclaimed. "I don't need a babysitter!"

"It isn't a babysitter," he reasoned. "It will be someone here to get your meals, take you on walks and help you into the shower."

"I don't need help going to the bathroom or showering," I snapped.

"I didn't mean that. I only meant to help you get back on your feet. You'll learn how to do all the things you used to do for yourself, but it's going to take time. A caregiver with experience in these matters will show you how to regain your independence."

My brain hung up on the word show. There would be no showing. "Show me, Dad, really?"

"I'm sorry. You know what I mean. This will be a good thing. You'll get to be away from me, and I won't be hovering all the time."

He was trying to make light of the situation. I wanted to laugh. I would have loved to laugh at his attempt to be funny. Somehow, I just couldn't find the energy. My face felt broken, like I would never smile again. "It isn't going to help," I muttered.

"It can't make things any worse," he replied. "I've already put an ad in the paper and have contacted a few agencies."

"Dad, I don't want a babysitter. I don't need a stranger hovering. It's only going to make things worse."

"I'm doing it anyway. We both need this."

"Whatever. I'm not going to let a nurse take care of me. I'm too old for that."

His answer was the door closing behind him, and I found myself plunged back into the aloneness that was becoming my new normal. I knew I was taking out my anger and hurt out on him and he didn't deserve it. It was my fault. I was the one who got in the car and hauled ass down the road. I was the one who didn't react fast enough. I had no one to blame but myself.

Before I could really work up a good case of self-guilt, there was another knock on the door. I would kill my dad if he had already hired a caregiver. "I'm sleeping."

"Bitch, don't lie to me."

I laughed. It was Melissa Shaw, my best friend in the whole world. Actually, my only friend. All my other friends had faded away. While I was in the hospital, my room had been flooded with cards. Once I moved out of the ICU, my room was flooded with flowers and I was hounded by visitors. That is until I turned into a pit viper, snapping at anyone who dared ask me how I was. No one wanted to be around me, and I didn't blame them.

"Did my dad call you? Did he demand you come over here and talk some sense into me?"

She laughed. "As if anyone could talk sense into you. You're about as stubborn as they come."

I heard her walking closer, followed by the sound of her dragging the other sitting chair over to the window.

"What brings you by then?" I asked.

"Uh, because you're my friend and I want to visit. You never answer your damn phone."

"It's weird to talk on the phone," I told her.

"You could do talk-to-text," she offered.

"I know what those end up looking like. I don't want to be featured on some talk-to-text fail page."

She slapped my knee. "As if I would do that. Why are you in here? Let's go outside."

"No."

"Oh. I get it now. You're pouting."

"I'm not pouting."

"What is going on? You sound even grumpier than usual."

I turned my face towards the window. I was a little self-conscious to have people look at me when I couldn't see them. I wasn't sure what my eyes were doing. Everyone told me I looked normal, but I had a feeling they were lying.

"My dad wants to hire a caregiver, also known as a babysitter. He can't deal with me. It's just like when I was a wild kid and they hired a nanny. I'm too fucking old for a babysitter."

"A caregiver is not a nanny," she pointed out. "This could be a good thing. It will give you and your dad a break from each other. You guys have never fought this much. You're both way stressed and could use a little break. You don't want me or him helping you, and that's understandable. Let someone that's paid to do it be your eyes."

Putting my head back, I imagined what the ceiling might look like. "I want my own eyes."

"I know, hon. I know. If any of us could give you back your sight, you have to know we would do it in a heartbeat."

"I know. I just hate this. Shit! I cannot tell you much I hate my life right now."

"I'm so sorry. And I know you hate when I say it, but you have to look on the bright side."

I scoffed. "What could possibly be the bright side of this? And, how the hell am I supposed to see the bright side when I can't even see!"

I heard her suck in a breath. "In the proverbial sense. What does the sun feel like on your face right now? What do you hear? I bet all of that is heightened without your sight."

"I could close my eyes and have the same experience."

She was quiet for several seconds. I knew I was being horrible. It was like I was trapped in the wrong body. I wasn't a bitch. I wasn't cranky. I wasn't blind. I was me, Gabrielle Sullivan, fun and flirty, a grab life by the horns and party kind of girl. I hated who I was. I hated being stuck in the body I was in. I just wanted out.

"Do you want to go outside for a bit?" she asked.

"No thank you."

"How about we go get some coffee?"

"No way. Definitely not."

"Bree, don't make this worse by confining yourself to this room. Coffee is still coffee whether you look at it or not. We can go down to the beach and stretch out on the sand. No swimming, just sunbathing. Vitamin D is good for the soul. It will help you heal."

"I am healed, Mel. I'm as healed as I'm going to get. My body isn't broken. My soul is."

"You're going to make me cry," she said. "I don't want to cry. I've cried enough. I refuse to let you do this to yourself. You have to get up. You have to live. I cannot live in this world without my best friend."

Turning to face her, I said, "Mel, I love you. I'm sorry I'm not my usual self. I don't know if I ever will be again. Right now, it's not looking like I will. I want to but it just isn't going to happen. I'm broken. Shattered actually, to be honest. My heart and soul have been crushed and to try and put it all back together feels impossible."

I heard her sob and knew I had made her cry. "It's killing me to see you this way, Bree. Please don't fade away on me. I know it seems impossible right now, but I'm here for you. I want to help you in any way I can. I know you're broken. Let me help put you back together again. Lean on me. You've always been the strong one. It's my turn."

"I'll try, but I'm not there yet. I'm still trying to remember how to smile."

"It'll come back. One day at a time. And, I'll be here. You can keep trying to get rid of me, but it isn't going to work. Now, you sit right here if you want, but I'm running to that coffee shop on the corner. I'm getting us a couple mochas and then me and you are going outside. I don't care if we sit by the pool or just walk around the yard, but we are going outside."

Clearly, I wasn't going to win. "Fine."

I heard her move and realized she was wearing jeans. I could hear the denim rub as she moved. "I'll be back. Don't even think about getting in that bed, because I will drag your ass out of here if I have to."

"I'll be right here. Trust me, I'm not going anywhere."

Ultimately, I knew I had a choice to be miserable or to accept my circumstances and move forward. While I knew I had the choice, and I knew what I should do, I couldn't quite take that first step forward. I had cement shoes on in a pool of blackness.

Chapter Six

Luke

GRADUALLY, I WAS FINDING my way around the area. I stuck pretty close to the neighborhoods near mine to do the bulk of my shopping. And I had submitted several more applications. No news yet, but I wasn't giving up hope. I couldn't afford to.

I parked my car in the parking lot of the grocery store I had been using of late. The ramen noodle thing was going to be a necessity if my situation didn't change soon. For now, I was getting by with a lot of rice and chicken. Heading inside, I grabbed the few things I needed and was on my way out to my car when I saw a man talking on his phone, headed directly for me.

He looked familiar. At first, I couldn't place him, then I remembered where I knew him from. The bar! He was walking towards me, appearing distracted. I wasn't in the mood for another confrontation and casually stepped to the side. The guy ended his call and stopped walking. He looked at me and I could see him trying to place me.

Fuck.

"Looking at something?" I snapped.

"You're that punk from the other day," he stated.

"Punk? I'm not the one getting sloppy drunk and starting fights in a bar."

He smirked. "You sure about that? If I remember right, you had a lot to say."

I shrugged, not about to back down. "Guy pushes me, there's something to be said."

He stared at me for several long seconds before a slow smile spread over his face. "You're not from around here."

"Nope."

"Do you live around here?"

"I don't swing that way," I shot back.

He chuckled, a deep throaty laugh. "Good. I don't want to fuck you. Where are you from?"

He seemed to relax. It wasn't like I had a lot of friends and couldn't turn down the chance of making one. "Dallas."

"No shit?"

I nodded. "No shit."

"Why in the hell are you out here in the slums of LA?"

"I guess because that's the best a guy like me could do," I said with a shrug. "Besides, I didn't know it was the slums when I rented the place."

He laughed. "Man, they are always getting people with those rental scams."

"Well, consider me got. I plan on looking for something else once I get a job."

"Let's grab a beer," he said.

I wasn't sure if he was genuinely nice or looking to set me up. "With your buddy?"

He grinned. "Nah. He's probably still sleeping that one off. His fiancé dumped him and eloped with one of his friends. He was in a bad way that night."

"Ouch. That sounds rough."

"It was. Come on. I owe you a beer for being a dick. I'm Austin Hampton by the way."

It was my turn to laugh. "Yes, you do owe me. Luke Turner," I said, reaching out to shake his hand.

I put my groceries in my car and followed him across the street to what could only be described as a yuppie bar, complete with micro-brews and kombucha.

"So, what brings you out to LA? You don't strike me as the kind of guy who has stars in his eyes."

"No stars. Just looking to start fresh somewhere sunny and warm."

"Isn't Dallas sunny?"

I had to smile. He had a point. "A little too sunny. It's hot as hell in the summer with humidity that will choke you. I lived there all my life and just didn't feel like doing it anymore."

He laughed. "Got it. What about family? Did you move out here with family or leave them behind?"

"I left them behind," I answered. "It's just me."

"Married?"

I shook my head. "Nope. You?"

"Hell no. Ever been married?"

"Nope. I've been working nonstop since I was about fifteen."

That seemed to intrigue him. "Really? Doing what?"

I cringed. "I got noticed at a beach and started modeling when I was still in high school. It paid the bills."

He burst into laughter. "I knew you were a pretty boy."

"Not a pretty boy," I argued. "What about you? Are you married?"

"Hell no, and it's going to stay that way for a while. What does your family think about you leaving the big Lone Star state?"

I shrugged. "I guess they aren't happy, but this is something I wanted to do."

He studied my face for a few seconds before nodding. "Got it. We won't talk about your family."

"What about you? You don't look like a guy from the slums. Is your family around?"

He let out a long sigh. "I'm not from LA. I buy up depressed property and turn it around. I live in Malibu."

"Ah, you're one of those guys that gentrifies a neighborhood so the residents can't afford it."

He grinned. "No. I clean up the buildings, make them habitable and then sell them. The rents do go up, but I haven't heard anyone complaining about having working AC and running water. The buildings I buy are dilapidated and unsafe. I guess some people might get pissy about me making them worth living in, but I don't care."

"So, you're a real estate tycoon?" I asked with surprise. I didn't take him for a wealthy guy, but now that I looked at him, I could see that refinement. He did a good job playing it down, but it was there.

He shrugged. "I don't know if I'm a tycoon, but I do alright."

He was humble and rich. I had met a few of his type in Dallas. The guys that still wore faded jeans and worn boots even after making it big. "Have you always lived here?"

"Yep. So, what do you do? You said you were looking for a job."

I hesitated. Austin was one of those manly men and I had a pretty good idea about how he would react when I told him what I did for a living. I had seen it a thousand times. Dallas wasn't exactly the kind of city where there were a lot of forward thinkers.

"Actually, I'm a nurse."

"No shit."

"No shit."

"Damn," he said, taking a drag from the beer. "That's cool. I've never met a guy nurse. Smart move though. I bet you meet a lot of hot nurses."

His reaction surprised me. "I have met a lot of hot nurses, but I'll be the first to admit, hot nurses like rich doctors. They don't want to hook up with a guy making the same thing they are."

He grimaced. "Ooh, that's painful. Isn't there some kind of nursing shortage though?"

"So, they say. The problem is registered nurses are all fighting for the same jobs. Hospital administration is tight. They'll put one RN on a shift and work the person to the bone. They fill in the holes with inexperienced aids and what not. It's the same wherever you go unless you manage to get in one of those private hospitals that can afford to pay decent wages."

"You need to look for jobs in Malibu. Lots of money up there. People up there pay good money to have their loved ones taken care of at home instead of some hospital."

"How far is it?" I asked, having no clue where Malibu was.

He shrugged. "Maybe an hour. You'll find a cushy job. Hell, I bet a lot of them are looking for live-in caregivers. They'll set you up in a pool house or guest house on the premises. You'll get all the perks of being wealthy with none of the drawbacks."

"Really?" I asked intrigued by the idea. "Is that a thing there? We had lots of caregiver jobs back home, but it was usually Medicaid and stuff. They don't pay worth shit and the jobs are undesirable."

He nodded. "No, I'm dead serious. I can ask around and see if someone is looking. What exactly do you do?"

"All of it. I'm a licensed registered nurse. I give meds, do IVs, you name it, I do it."

"Oh shit, you're an actual nurse, like saving lives and shit?"

I laughed. "What'd you think I was? Is there a fake nurse?"

He shrugged. "I don't know. I guess I was thinking you were too pretty to be an actual nurse. Did you work in a hospital?"

"I did. I worked in the emergency department."

"Damn, I bet that was exciting."

"Exciting is a relative term. It was a lot of babies with coughs and homeless people with diabetes or some other ailment."

"Gory?" he asked with interest.

I laughed. "It can be. You kind of learn to tune that out. You look past the ick."

"That's cool, and an admirable job. I'm too fucking selfish to get my hands dirty doing that shit. How long have you been in town?"

"Almost two weeks."

He slowly nodded. "You'll have to come up and hit the beach with me. Ladies for days wearing very tiny bikinis. That's what you're really in LA for, right?"

I grinned. "The thought had crossed my mind a time or two."

He wrote down his number on a napkin. "Give me a call sometime, we'll hang out and I'll show you why you came out here."

I tore off a piece of the same napkin and jotted down my number. "Call me if you find anyone looking for a home nurse. I don't necessarily need to live on the premises but if that's what they want, I'll do it."

"I'll do that. I've got to run, but I'll be in touch."

I waved, finished my beer and headed back across the street to my car. Once I had my meager groceries put away, I sat down with my laptop and widened my job search to include Malibu. I browsed through the job listings and didn't find any hospitals or clinics.

There was an ad for a caregiver for a young woman. I immediately dismissed the ad and kept looking. I wasn't interested in getting myself into a situation that was almost exactly what I was trying to get away from. I was probably being prejudiced but it was instinct. Self-preservation told me to avoid women. I had a soft spot for women in that I felt like I *had* to take care of them.

I wanted to be a nurse, not necessarily the guy taking care of a broken woman. When nothing else turned up in my search, I went back to the ad for a caregiver for a disabled young lady. It wasn't my ideal job, but it paid extremely well. The ad asked for someone energetic with a flexible schedule.

Clearly, I could do that, but did I want to? There wasn't a lot of information about what all the job included. I had worked private gigs before where I was required to do cooking and cleaning as well as take care of the patient. Usually, the situations tended to be families needing an elderly loved one taken care of. Again, probably about my least favorite clientele.

"Do you want to stay or go?" I asked myself, my finger hovering over the mouse.

I didn't want to go home. I was a professional and I could handle a tough customer. With the wage the ad offered, I could afford to move out of the place I was in. That was the first goal. I would get some local experience and keep applying for jobs that were more my speed.

"Fuck it," I said and clicked on the information.

There was an email address and phone number listed. I quickly sent over my resume with a quick cover letter before I could change my mind. I had to start somewhere. How bad could it be?

Chapter Seven

Bree

I HAD MADE IT OUT OF my room and was sitting in the solarium. It had been a special addition to the mansion and my mother's favorite room. It had always been a place of comfort for me. I had managed to find the room on my own with only a few minor bumps into the furniture. One of the housekeepers had brought me some cold lemonade and little sandwiches.

They were all tiptoeing around me. No one knew what to say or how to act. It was one of the reasons I preferred to stay in my room. I didn't want to make anyone uncomfortable. If I was holed up in my room, they would leave me alone. When I was out and about, the staff was around, asking if I needed anything or offering to help.

I didn't want help.

"Hey," my dad's voice startled me.

"What?"

"I've got an interview in a couple minutes. Do you want to sit in?"

I shook my head. "No."

He sighed. "I think it would be a good idea for you to be a part of the interview process. After all, it's you who will be spending time with whoever we hire."

"I don't need a babysitter."

"I'm hiring someone," he said and walked out.

And I knew that he would. Whoever he hired better be ready for me, because I wasn't going to be a willing participant in my dad's little party. I didn't need a babysitter. He thought some stranger was going to waltz in, wave a magic wand and I would be back to my old self. It wasn't going to happen.

The doorbell rang, followed by the sound of the housekeeper's footsteps. I imagined my dad was in his study. Though I strained my ears trying to hear—the study was too far away. I focused on the feeling of the sun and the scent of the dirt in the potted plants I knew to be scattered around the room. I could picture the big palm in the corner with a variety of succulents on tables and in the window sills.

My days were spent picturing rooms, things, and people in my mind. I thought about my future. I thought about how I would age. I wouldn't even know what I looked like. I wouldn't know if my brown hair was turning gray or if I was getting age spots. I assumed I would be able to feel the wrinkles, but I couldn't say for sure.

"Bree," I heard my father call out.

"What?" I snapped.

He cleared his throat. "I've brought Mrs. Patterson with me. We've been talking and she would like to meet you."

I was going to kill him. "Great," I muttered. "Here I am."

"Hi Bree," the woman said in a friendly voice.

I was pegging her to be in her fifties, maybe even older. I realized I couldn't know for sure without seeing her face. "Hello."

"Your father says you are in need of some help around the house."

"My father is mistaken."

"Oh," the woman said.

"Bree, we've talked about this."

"No, you've talked about this," I snapped. "I told you I don't need a babysitter."

"I'm not a babysitter," Mrs. Patterson answered in a calm voice. "I would be here to help you do the things you used to do. We can take walks, go shopping, whatever you like."

"I would like to be left alone. Can you help with that?"

I heard a sharp intake of breath and was sure I wasn't the only one. "Gabrielle!"

"I don't want a stupid caregiver, babysitter or whatever you want to call it."

"I'm so sorry," he said. "I'll walk you out."

Hearing their footsteps recede, I sighed with relief. I wasn't in the mood to entertain someone or pretend to be happy about the idea of getting a babysitter. It was only a few minutes later when I heard my father's footsteps coming back.

"We need to talk," he said, pulling a chair across the room.

"I don't want to talk. I just want to be alone."

"We're going to talk about this," he said, "whether you like it or not." He spoke in a familiar tone that said he meant business.

"What is there to talk about?"

"You need help," he bluntly said.

"I don't need some lady coming in here and acting like she's my friend or trying to be my mother!"

The silence was palpable. "She isn't trying to be your mother."

"Good, because I don't need someone trying to take her place."

"Bree, no one will ever take your mother's place," he said, with the familiar sadness that I heard in his voice whenever we talked about her.

I gulped down the lump in my throat. "I don't want anyone."

"We need someone."

"We did fine after mom died. I was a lot younger back then and we managed. I know I'm basically an invalid, but I can't deal with someone coming in here. I just can't."

"Don't use that word. And if she were here, she would want to do the best for you. She would say we needed to hire a team of people."

I scoffed. "No, she would take care of me herself."

"I'm trying, Bree. I swear I'm trying. You don't want me to take care of you. When you were little and I could hear you in your room crying after she died, it was the same thing. You hated the idea of me coddling you. You were always so strong. You're still that same strong girl you were back then but I know you're hurting. I know you need help and I just don't know what to do."

"Just let me get through this," I begged. "Just leave me alone and let me get through it."

"Bree, that's just it. You aren't getting through. You're stuck. You're weighed down and this isn't doing you any good. Remember after she died how we both kind of withdrew. We didn't leave the house. We didn't have friends over. We wrapped ourselves up in grief and it nearly took us both down. I've learned my lesson. I won't let that happen again."

Hearing him talk about that period in our lives when nothing made sense and pain was all I knew, was a sober reminder of all we had been through. "I just need some time."

"You can't take any more time. The longer you stay down, the harder it will be to get back up. If I have to be the bad guy, I will. I'm not going to lose you."

The emotion in his voice tugged at my heartstrings. "You're not losing me."

His hand touched mine. "I almost did, Bree. I can't tell you what it was like to watch you day in and day out while you were in that coma. The doctors were not optimistic and I kept trying to figure out how I was ever going to move on with my life if you didn't come out of it. I couldn't have. You're all I have in this world Bree. I cannot lose you. While you might be physically here, I can feel you slipping away."

My heart hurt to think of what he had gone through in those days while I had been blissfully unaware of his pain or even my own. My body had healed while I had been out of it. Everything except my vision. He had been the one to suffer—not me.

"I'm sorry," I blurted out, tears streaming down my cheeks. "I don't mean to be such a pain in the ass. I can hear myself doing it and I want to stop but it just comes out. I don't feel like myself at all. Instead, I feel like I've been possessed by this bitter woman who won't let me go."

He chuckled. "Well, we need to kick that bitch to the curb. The way we do that is to find your happiness again. We have to tap into that inner strength I know you have down inside you. I truly believe having someone around to take you places and help you regain some independence is going to help. I know you. I know how tough you are. Once you get started, there will be no stopping you."

A small laugh erupted from my throat. It took me by surprise, the sound was foreign to my ears. "I want to believe you, I really do, but this is all so overwhelming."

"I know it is. I can't say I know what you're going through, but I know it's hard. I'm here for you. It's me and you. It's always been me and you against the world. We can get through this if we stick together. We don't have anyone else we can count on."

He was right. "I'll try. I'll do better."

"Good, I have more interviews scheduled for tomorrow. I really think it would be beneficial for you to meet these people."

I shook my head. "No. You meet them. You interview and you read their body language. If they get past you, then I'll talk to them. No old people, please. I don't want to feel like I'm hanging out with my grandmother."

He chuckled. "Deal."

"Thanks, Dad. I know you're trying. I'll try too, but I'm making no promises. I'm still really angry."

"That is to be expected."

"Has Nate called anymore?"

"I'm sorry, pumpkin," he started. "The last time I talked to him, he was headed out of town. He sent his love and said he would call you when he got back to town. He sent more flowers but I didn't bother bringing them into your room since you said you couldn't stand the smell."

"No, I can't. I never want to smell flowers again. I got enough of that in the hospital."

"People were just trying to let you know they were thinking about you."

I nodded. "I know, and that was nice, but being in that tiny hospital room surrounded with what felt like a million flowers, I've had my fill."

"The therapist did say your senses would be enhanced."

I made a choking sound. "Maybe that's true, I don't know, but I never want to smell flowers again."

"Noted. I'll let you be now. You know what to do if you need anything."

"I do. Thank you for being so patient with me. I'm going to try to do better."

"It's all good. I'll see you at dinner."

When I felt him leave, I finally released the tension I'd been holding in. My father had no idea what had happened between me and Nate that night before the accident. I didn't see the need to tell him. Nate had apparently visited often while I had been in the coma. My dad didn't need to know the guy he thought of as his son-in-law was already no longer a part of my life.

What I knew for certain was that I needed to get through this murky pit before I could ever begin to deal with Nate. At least with a babysitter hanging around, I could have him or her run interference for me. They could tell Nate that I was asleep or busy doing some therapy.

Quickly, I pushed aside any thoughts of Nate. I needed to focus on me. Clearly, I couldn't keep going like this. I had pushed my dad to the limit, I could sense that. I knew he was suffering and no matter how cranky I felt for myself, I didn't want to hurt him. I would do better for his sake if not for my own.

He wasn't exactly a young and I didn't need to stress him out and give him a heart attack or stroke. He was my reason for getting better. Not getting better, but coping better. At the very least, I could learn to fake it when he was around. Like he said, we were all we had. We'd been through hell together once, we could do it again.

Chapter Eight

Luke

NERVOUS AS HELL, THAT'S how I was feeling. I wasn't even sure I wanted the job, but here I was, pulling into the gated driveway of what had to be one of the biggest houses I had ever seen. Austin wasn't lying when he said there was a lot of money in Malibu. I had apparently been living under a rock and didn't realize just how many celebrities called the place home. It was an exclusive community with lots of gates and a ton of security.

I felt out of place in my little Maxima as I rolled up the driveway. I wasn't sure where I was supposed to park. There wasn't a valet or designated parking spots, so I just found a place that looked kind of out of the way and shut off the engine.

Clearly I didn't belong here. That was the thought that dominated all the other increasingly frantic thoughts floating through my head. I did not belong in a house like this. I turned to look up at the massive home that stretched out forever in both directions before curving in what I assumed was a U shape. Or maybe it was an L. I couldn't say for sure from this angle.

It was massive, I was certain about that. Getting out of the car, I walked over the cobblestone driveway and up to the front door and immediately rang the bell. Usually I knocked on doors to keep from disturbing anyone with a door chime, but in a house that big, I seriously doubted anyone would hear me knocking.

An older woman wearing black slacks and a pretty blue blouse answered the door. "Can I help you?" she asked.

"I'm here for an interview," I said.

"Ah, you're here to see Paul. Come in and I'll show you to the sitting room."

I nodded, having no idea what a sitting room was. I assumed it was
a living room, or hell, maybe mansions like this had something akin to
a waiting room, I didn't know.

"Can I get you a drink?" she asked.

"No, thank you. I'm fine."

I barely heard the question, being too caught up in the lavish décor.
Never had a seen a staircase so large. It was actually two staircases. One
on the left and one on the right of the massive foyer, and they gently
curved their way up to the second floor.

There was a massive chandelier hanging over the area, so huge it
seemed a little scary to be under. She led me to an open room in the
middle, almost directly under the stairs. It was decorated in pale blues
and creamy whites. The ceilings were ridiculously high, and everything
sparkled and shone. The Carrara marble was the real thing I was sure,
and I felt like I should have left my shoes at the door.

The bright white floors, the clean white walls and the huge windows with gauzy curtains made the room feel ten times bigger than it
actually was. I was in awe. I had never seen anything so grand in my life.

"Have a seat," the woman directed. "Paul will be right in."

Taking a seat on the baby blue couch, I just tried to keep from mess-
ing anything up. My eyes roamed around the room, taking in a painting
of the ocean hanging over the mantle of the fireplace in the room. I assumed it was done by some fancy artist and cost more than I would ever
make in a lifetime. There were other paintings on the walls, small and
of various outdoor settings. There was a huge bouquet of fresh flowers
sitting on a small table. It added color to the room, but they looked a
little out of place. They weren't a usual fixture I was guessing. Someone

had been sent the flowers, likely the person I was supposed to be caring for—assuming I got the job.

It wasn't garish at all, but the house obviously belonged to someone very wealthy. The opulence was everywhere, although quite tastefully done. I couldn't imagine living in such a big house. How could a person actually ever use the entire house?

"Hello," a man's voice cut into my musings.

I jumped up from the couch. "Hello. I'm Luke Turner."

The man looked to be in his late forties, early fifties maybe. He was tall and appeared to be in good shape. He extended his hand, his dark eyes full of wisdom and what I sensed was pain.

"Paul Sullivan," he announced. "Have a seat, please."

I took my seat once again. Paul sat on the matching sofa directly across from me. I studied his mannerisms. He had a thick head of salt and pepper hair and was wearing a casual business shirt and slacks. He was the kind of man that screamed money, but in the most casual way. There was an air about him that unquestionably established that he was a powerful man.

"Thank you for giving me the opportunity to meet you in person," I said, suddenly very nervous.

Paul offered a friendly smile. "It's my pleasure."

I relaxed a little. The smile felt genuine, and Paul seemed like a nice guy. Reserved, but nice. "You have a beautiful home."

"Thank you. I'd like to talk to you a little about your experience, but first I'd like to explain to you what kind of job this is and what it isn't. My daughter is young, healthy and active. At least, she used to be. She was recently in an accident and has lost her sight. She is physically able to do everything on her own. However, this is all new to her and I need someone that can be here for her without being in her way. Does that make sense?"

I slowly nodded. "You are looking for more of a companion versus an actual nurse?"

He smiled. "I guess you could say that, yet I definitely need some-one with professional expertise and experience. She needs to regain her independence. I will tell you that she isn't looking forward to having someone around, but at this point I don't feel comfortable leaving her alone all day. We have staff, but I need someone that is focused on help-ing her."

"I see." My curiosity was piqued. He was describing her as an inde-pendent invalid. I needed to know which she was.

"Her name is Gabrielle but she goes by Bree. She is full of life. At least, she used to be. Since the accident, she's been severely depressed. She's only recently moved back into the house. She needs to relearn her way around the house and I would like her to get outside. That's the most important thing."

"I can do that," I said, still not entirely sure why he was looking for a medical professional when a simple support person would seemingly fit the bill.

"I'd like you to meet her, and see if she is willing to work with you. I will confess that she has met other candidates and wasn't thrilled."

I softly laughed. "Understandable. I'd like to meet her too, and we can decide how to move forward. I was under the impression the job was more of something that required skilled nursing services."

Paul let out a sigh. "I need someone that is professionally trained, and honestly, I do worry about her. She was in a coma for weeks after suffering a very serious head injury. We were warned that there could be seizures. I'm not comfortable with just anyone watching her at this point."

"I understand, sir. That makes good sense to me."

"Would you like to meet her now?"

"Sure."

"She's in the solarium," he said, getting to his feet.

I wasn't even entirely sure what a solarium was, though I was about to find out. We headed down a wide hall with various doors and open archways that led into what looked like more living rooms to me. We walked towards a set of French doors at the end of the hall with bright sunlight spilling out.

"Bree," Paul said, slowly opening the door. "I'd like you to meet someone."

"Again?" I heard a soft voice say.

I walked in behind Paul and saw a young woman with her back to us as she stood in front of a window. If I didn't know she was blind, I would have assumed she was looking out at the manicured garden with a wide array of blooms behind the bench sitting just beyond the window.

She slowly turned to face us, and I don't know why I was surprised, but I was. She was a beautiful woman. Her brown hair was perfectly straight, hanging midway down her back. Her skin had the faded remnants of a tan and was perfectly smooth without any blemishes. When her father had said she was in an accident, I had wrongly assumed she would still have some kind of physical scars.

Endless beauty is what I saw. She had an athletic figure, thin but muscular. She was wearing a pair of yoga pants and little tank top that showed off her perfect figure. The lack of makeup was likely due to her inability to put it on herself, but I didn't mind it a bit. She was perfect just as she was. Her crystal clear blue eyes were unseeing, but absolutely stunning.

"Hello," I said, after the awkward pause in conversation.

"Bree, this is Luke."

"Hi Bree," I said, watching her reaction.

She didn't look happy to be meeting me, and I remembered Paul saying she was reluctant to have anyone around in general.

"Hi Luke," she finally answered. "I suppose my father told you all about my woes."

"He said you might need someone around, not to help you, but just to keep you company at times. I imagine it can get lonely in this big house."

Paul smiled, encouraging my soft approach to his daughter.

"He said that, huh?" she asked, looking a little irritated.

I could feel her agony and see that she was suffering, though it wasn't a physical pain. I could fix a broken body, but I couldn't fix a broken soul. I imagined she had once been a very active person and her new situation was wreaking havoc on her mental state.

"I was thinking maybe you and I could grab some coffee tomorrow or something. We could talk, get to know each other a bit and see if this is a good fit."

Paul scowled at me, but when Bree's facial expression changed from irritated to intrigued, he relaxed a little. "You want to have coffee?" she asked.

"Sure. I would suggest a beer, but your dad is standing two feet away from me and I don't get the feeling he would appreciate it."

Paul chuckled. "No, he would not."

Bree made a face. "I'm not a child, Dad. We've talked about this."

"I know, I know. Would you like to do that?"

Bree hesitated. "I don't think so," she muttered. "We don't need to get to know each other. My father is looking to hire a babysitter. We don't have to be friends."

Her biting remark didn't really surprise me. People that were sick or in pain tended to be cranky and lashed out at the first person they encountered. That tended to be nurses a lot of the time. "Alright, that's understandable."

"Bree," her father hissed.

"It's okay, really. I get it. It was nice to meet you, Bree. I'll let you get back to what you were doing."

She scoffed. "Nothing. That's what I was doing. Absolutely nothing."

I slowly nodded, looking at Paul who had a pained expression on his face. I walked out and waited for Paul. He joined me in the hall and led me back towards the front door. "I'm sorry," he apologized. "She's really struggling."

"I get it. I'm not sure she's ready for a companion, a nurse or as she said, a babysitter. You might need to look for someone with a sterner approach. That's not me."

Paul shook his head. "No. We tried that route, it didn't work at all. I think she would warm up to you. You're closer to her age and you can get her out of the house and the funk she's in. I'd like to offer you the job."

I had a feeling his daughter would strongly object to his decision. "Can I think about it and get back to you tonight?" I asked.

He smiled. "Yes. She's a handful, but I promise, once you get to know her, she's the sweetest girl you'll ever meet."

"I don't doubt that at all. Thank you for the chance to meet with you both."

I walked out of the house and headed for my car. Another car pulled in behind me, a flashy red convertible. A young lady with long blonde hair and even longer legs climbed out, looking me up and down. I assumed it was another one of Paul's daughters. I offered her a smile and got into my car. I wasn't sure what I was going to do. Bree reminded me a lot of my mother in the sense that she didn't have physical pain, but emotional pain. I wasn't sure I was ready to jump right back into a situation like that.

Chapter Nine

Bree

"WOMAN!" I HEARD MEL shout in the distance.

I shook my head. She was very comfortable in our house. I heard my father direct her to the solarium. She came bursting in like the world was on fire.

"Slow down, turbo," I told her when she breezed in, actually creating a wind.

"Oh my goodness!" she exclaimed.

"What?" I asked, touching my hair and wondering if there was something grievously wrong with my appearance.

"That guy. Who was that guy?"

"Blind girl here, don't know what guy you're talking about."

She gave an exaggerated sigh. "He was so dreamy."

"Who? Who was dreamy?"

"The guy that was leaving as I came in."

That intrigued me. "Luke?"

"You know him?" she gasped.

"If he was leaving when you came in, it might have been the caregiver my dad is trying to hire. I talked to him for like a minute. I thought he sounded youngish."

"Girl, he's hot. Very, very hot. He could be my nurse any day of the week."

I smirked. "What does he look like? Be real and don't embellish."

As expected, she let out a long, exaggerated sigh. "I will tell you, but only if you agree to go get coffee with me. We can go to that one place with outdoor seating. No one will bother you."

"That was very scandalous."

She laughed. "Come on. You're dressed and ready. Let's go."

"I don't even know if I match," I complained.

"You do. You have on black pants and a purple tank. Your flats work with the outfit. Now, no more excuses. I need caffeine and I can tell you all about Mr. McHottie."

"Just because you add a mick to the front of a name, it doesn't make him hot," I said in a dry tone.

Her soft giggle filled the room. "Trust me, I don't need to add anything to his name to make him hot. He is the very definition."

"You're just trying to tease me in order to get me to go."

"Girl, I'm giving you incentive. One way or another I'm dragging you out of this house. You can make it easy or hard, but I will resort to hair pulling if that's what it takes."

I groaned, throwing my arms out. "Fine. I'll go."

She clapped her hands before looping her arm through my elbow and leading me out of the room. We stopped by my father's study to tell him we were going out, which of course thrilled him to no end. Mel did a great job of letting me get in her car on my own. I closed my eyes and leaned my head back against the seat. It felt good to have the wind in my hair as we sailed down the road with the top down.

When we got to the coffee place, she led me to a table outside on the patio. I could smell the ocean and feel the slight bit of moisture in the air. I knew exactly what place we were at. It was kind of out of the way. There was little chance we would run into anyone I knew. I was grateful for that. I wasn't ready to have other people see me, especially when I couldn't see them and their reactions.

"Here you go," Mel's voice came from my right.

"Thank you." I very slowly reached forward until I felt the cup with my fingertips. I grabbed it and took a sip. It was strange to be sitting at a coffee shop and drinking a latte without seeing anything.

"Alright, so... your hot nurse," she started.

"He isn't my nurse. Not yet. I don't know if my dad hired him."

"He should. He's hot."

I groaned. "I don't think that is a requirement to be a good nurse or caregiver and I'm certain my father didn't add it to the advertisement."

"Shh, let me tell you about him. He's tall and has kind of a swimmer's build. You know the type. Broad shoulders, lean and muscular. Sandy blonde hair, cut in a perfect good boy cut. I could do without that. I like my men a little more edgy. He has a very Viking look about him. A strong, square jaw and a very clean cut, boy next door thing going. I bet he's great in bed."

My mouth dropped open. "Mel! My goodness. You always look at men and think about sex. There is something wrong with you."

"The fact that you don't is what's wrong."

I laughed. The sound escaped my mouth before I even had time to think about it. It shocked the hell out of me. It had been too long since I had laughed like that. "You are the horniest woman I have ever met."

"I am. I don't mind. So, did you talk to him?"

I shrugged. "Briefly."

"Well? What did you think?"

"He was nice. He asked if I wanted to grab coffee."

"That's different. What did you say? Wait, don't tell me; you told him no."

I cringed. "I didn't know what to say. I don't know why he wanted to get coffee. We're not dating. We're not getting to know each other."

She sighed. "Would it be so bad to have someone around that you actually like? He sounds like he just wants to get to know you in order to help you better. The goal is to help you get back on your feet, right?"

"Yes," I answered. "But why do we need to be friends?"

"Because if he knows you, he'll know what you need. He'll be able to read your moods. Like me. I know you and can see when you're happy or sad or itching to get out of the house, even if you say you don't want to."

I took another drink. "He probably would be better to hang out with than the old lady my dad introduced me to."

"Yes, he would, and I bet he would like to go to the beach. Oh, maybe you guys could do one of those tandem bike things. He can be the eyes and you can be the muscle. Although, I think he would be able to drive you all around."

I smiled. "Riding a bike would be cool, but a tandem? That's so cheesy."

"And fun."

"I don't know. I don't want to be pitied."

"Then don't be pitiful," she retorted. "Get up, brush yourself off and let's figure out how this works."

"How this works? You mean me being blind?"

"Yes," she answered. "You're blind and that's the new normal. I'm by your side and ready to learn how to navigate this new world. I know things will be different. It won't be the same, I get that, but you and me are a team. We can do this."

"You sound like my dad now."

She laughed. "Because we both love you and want to see you through this. I'm not going to lie, I know this isn't going to be easy. But it's time to step up and move on."

I felt a familiar squeeze in my chest. It was the tightness that always preceded a panic attack. "Anytime I look towards my future, my dark future, I panic. Part of me is still in denial. I keep hoping I'll wake up and it will all have been a nightmare. If I accept that I'm blind, then I have to live in that world forever."

"I'm sorry," she whispered. "I don't know what else to say. I don't know what to do. All I can do is be here for you.

"And you are doing a great job of that and I do appreciate you being here for me."

"Good. Now, let's talk about the sexy nurse some more."

I laughed again and felt like the pressure valve had been released somehow. Like the cork that had been preventing me from laughing and smiling had been removed and I could breathe again.

"Okay, I'll call my dad and tell him I will agree to having the guy around on a trial basis. I don't want to get everybody too excited, just in case it doesn't work out."

"This guy, I've got a good feeling about him," she said.

"You saw him for two seconds," I quipped. "How could you possibly know?"

"Because I know you and I know what you like. This guy looked tough. He looks like he could put up with your little temper tantrums, but if you get too out of hand, he could easily bend you over his knee and give you a good spanking."

I burst into laughter again. "If he touches me, I will knock him right on his ass. I don't have to be able to see him to do that."

"See, he's already got you back in fighting form."

"What if we don't get along? Like you said, I can be a real pain in the ass."

She giggled. "He's being paid to be your buddy. That should be incentive enough to stick it out with you."

I grinned. "Sheesh. I better tell my dad to pay him really well."

"This is going to be good for you. I think it's the first big step in the right direction. I know you. You're a stubborn woman and once you get going, there will be no stopping you. This guy is going to give you a push in the right direction."

"You sound pretty confident about that."

"I am. Call your dad right this minute. We don't want this one to get away. An old lady will not be good for you. You need someone to push you in the right direction."

"Shove," I said. "Shove hard."

"Call," she ordered.

I fished out my phone, used my thumb to unlock it and asked Siri to call dad. He answered on the first ring. "Are you okay?" he asked, out of breath.

"I'm good, Dad. I'm good. I just wanted to let you know I'd like you to hire that nurse guy, Luke."

"Really?"

"Yes, really."

"I'll call him right now," he said with excitement.

I ended the call and put my phone away. "I cannot believe I just agreed to have a babysitter."

"It's not a babysitter. It's someone to be your buddy and help you get back into the land of the living. Me and your dad, we're too close to the situation. You need someone that can be more objective and push you a bit, but differently than we do, because heaven knows that's not working."

With a bit of a grin, I slowly nodded. "I really hope you're right, Mel."

"What do you have to lose?"

"This is true. I've already lost just about everything."

She reached out and touched my hand. "And now it's time to start taking it back."

We finished our coffees and she took me back home. I told her I could get to the door on my own. She argued, but let me go. I could hear the engine of her car and knew she was watching me, but I didn't mind. I made it inside, taking a minute to orient myself to where I was. Slowly, I was learning how to navigate without sight.

"Ah, you're back," my father said from my left.

I turned towards him. "I'm back."

"I called Luke and offered the job, but I'm sorry, he turned it down. He didn't think it was a good fit."

I couldn't believe what I was hearing. "Did you offer him good money?"

"I did," he answered.

"Oh." I stood, unmoving for several seconds. "I'm going to my room to lay down for a bit."

"Do you need—"

"No," I said, stopping him before he could finish his sentence. "I can do it."

I slowly found my way to my room. I couldn't explain why I was so upset that Luke had declined the job, but I blamed Mel. She'd gotten me excited for the chance to find a new normal. Apparently, fate had other plans.

Chapter Ten

Luke

I KNEW I WAS PROBABLY shooting myself in the foot by rejecting the job, but I couldn't do it. There were too many similarities between my mom and the young woman. I didn't want to get caught up in an emotional trap. I didn't know her story, but it sounded like a sad one. I could see the trauma in her. I could see the way she held herself and knew she was struggling to come to terms with her situation.

That was a lot of emotional baggage and I wasn't qualified to deal with it. I didn't want to fall into the same old routine I had been in with my mother. I didn't want to deal with the emotional abuse and then find myself bending over backwards to try and make her feel better. It would end up being one of those unhealthy relationships.

There was also the little problem of my attraction towards her. I couldn't be attracted to a client. I had worked with beautiful women in the past, but there was something different about Bree. I could see that spark of life still in her, and I wanted to be the one to help her find it and blossom.

"Stay away," I told myself, needing to hear the words.

Getting emotionally involved would be a mistake. I knew I would want to fix her. I would invest my whole being into making her better at a great cost to myself. I pushed thoughts of Bree to the side and focused on finding a new job. I applied to a couple more, sent follow-up emails to a few of the hospitals and then called it a day.

When my phone rang, I assumed it would be my mother again. The woman had stepped up her game and had been calling nonstop. But this wasn't my mother calling. It was a number I didn't recognize, but I knew it was from the LA area. It could be a job.

"Hello," I answered in my best professional voice, which unintentionally came out a little deeper than usual.

"Is this Luke Turner?" a woman asked.

"It is. Who's calling?"

"This is Bree Sullivan. We met yesterday."

As if I could forget. "Hello Bree."

"I was wondering if the offer to grab a coffee still stands."

That was not what I expected. "Um, sure, but I don't know if your dad told you, but I'm not going to be able to take the job."

"He did. You'll have to pick me up though, my car was totaled in the accident."

I blinked. Her car was totaled. That's why she couldn't drive? Then I realized she was making a joke. A very dark humored joke, but a joke, nonetheless.

"I can pick you up. When?"

"Are you doing anything now? My schedule is pretty clear as of late."

I had to bite back the laugh again. "Turns out, mine is wide open as well. I'll be there in an hour, maybe a little longer."

She groaned. "Then you'll be taking me to lunch."

That time I did laugh. "Okay. I can take you to lunch, but it's got to be cheap, I'm unemployed."

I heard her laugh and knew I was in trouble. But maybe now that I wasn't her nurse, we could be something else. I put the phone down and headed into the bedroom to take the world's fastest shower before changing into some clean clothes. I stopped when I checked my reflection in the mirror for the third time.

She couldn't see me. Why was I getting all dolled up for a woman that couldn't see me? I shook my head, grabbed my phone and car keys and headed out. I wasn't sure what made her change her mind about grabbing coffee, but I was interested in getting to know her a little better.

When I arrived, her father let me in. He was very happy to know she had called me. Bree gave me the name of a café. I put it in my GPS and off we went. When we got to the café, I did my best to guide her without smothering her. I placed one hand on the small of her back while I walked alongside her, navigating around the tables and other diners. She insisted we eat outside on the patio, which was fine by me.

"What made you change your mind?" I asked her. She was wearing dark sunglasses, shielding those beautiful eyes from me. She looked like a movie star. A gorgeous movie star.

She shrugged. "I guess I had some time to think about it. The way I see it, I'm either stuck with you, or I'm stuck with some old hag. You're the lesser of two evils."

I laughed. "That's flattering. I think."

"Sorry, I don't gush. I don't use pretty words or massage egos."

"Good to know."

"Is that rude? I'm sorry. This is me. I'm a little raw and unfiltered. I don't mean to be mean, but I'm kind of struggling to find myself."

"This is you, raw and unfiltered. I don't think that's a bad thing. It's kind of refreshing. I've only been in town a couple weeks and I have discovered there is a thick layer of fake covering the bulk of the people I have met. I have never seen so many fake smiles and fake b—" I stopped talking. The woman had put me at ease and I almost said something completely inappropriate. "Sorry."

She burst into laughter. The sound was refreshing and natural. "Fake boobs, that's what you were going to say, wasn't it. I cannot believe you almost said that."

"I'm really sorry," I said again. I was mortified. "I swear, that isn't how I normally talk to clients."

"But I'm not a client. Not yet."

"I turned down the job," I reminded her.

"You did, and I want to know why. Is it me?"

"No," I answered too quickly.

"It's me. I was a bitch to you. Truthfully, I was less of a bitch to you than the others."

I chuckled. "Good to know."

"I'd like you to reconsider the job. I need someone young enough to keep up with me. And if you're laughing about keeping up with blind me, you can wipe the smile right off your face. Once I get my bearings, I'm going to be off and running. Probably running into things, but running nonetheless."

"I believe you. I have no doubt in my mind you'll be on your way in no time."

She took a drink from her soda. "But yet you didn't say yes."

"I'm sorry, but I'm a nurse and I'm not sure this is the right fit. You don't need a nurse."

"No, but I need someone that can push me to try harder and someone that I have something in common with."

I grinned. "What do we have in common?"

"You're twenty-eight. I asked my dad. We're born in the same decade. That's more than what I have in common with the others that have applied for the position. I know my dad and I'm sure he made you a generous offer. But I'll make him pay you more."

"You drive a hard bargain," I said with a laugh.

"That's something you should know about me. I'm tenacious."

I mulled it over and decided it was a job and I needed the money. Seeing her how she was now changed my initial opinion. Maybe she wasn't the needy, emotional woman I had met before. Maybe there was a little more to her.

"Okay," I finally said.

She grinned. "Great. You'll start tomorrow, and before you say you can't, you already told me you had a clear schedule."

I laughed again. "Damn, you are a little intimidating."

"When I know what I want, I go after it. It feels good to be assertive again."

"How do you know I'm what you want?"

She shrugged. "I like your laugh."

I had a feeling we were on to something good. We ate our lunch before I took her home with the promise that I would be back in the morning. I was thrilled to have a job. A very good paying job at that. Depending on how things went, I could be out of the dump I was in very soon.

When I showed up to work the following morning, it was not what I expected. Paul was going to be gone all day. It was just going to be me and Bree.

"So, what would you like to do today?" I asked.

"You've been here ten minutes, slow down a little."

I laughed. "I like to be on the move. Can you give me a tour of this place? It's huge and like nothing I have ever seen."

"Uh, I'm not sure I can give you a tour. I can't see, remember?"

I reached for her hand. The moment I touched her there was a sizzle of electricity that hummed through my veins. She jerked away. I had a feeling she felt it as well.

"You live here. I bet you know your way around. What about outside? Do you guys have a pool?"

"Of course, we have a pool," she snapped.

I ignored the attitude. "Let's take a walk outside."

She let out a breath. "Fine."

Walking alongside her, I was ready to stop her from running into a wall if it looked like that was going to happen. It was slow going, but she was doing it all on her own. "I'll get the door."

"I can do it myself," she snapped.

"I'm sure you can, but I'm a gentleman and I don't care if you have twenty-twenty vision, I'm still going to open doors."

She groaned. "You're one of those guys."

"If you mean a Texas gentleman, then yes, I am."

She snorted, but said nothing else about it. I followed her as she walked down a stone path through the garden. "Am I close to the archway?" she asked.

I looked around. "Uh yes, on the right."

"We go through there," she instructed.

I reached down and grabbed her hand again. She jerked it away. "Don't touch me!"

"Whoa," I said, stepping back and putting my hands up. "I wasn't trying to do anything. I just wanted to guide you around the patio furniture. The pool is about fifty feet in front of you."

"I know where the pool is. I don't need to be coddled."

"I'm not coddling you," I assured her. "I'm by your side but this is all you."

She exhaled a breath. "Fine, but don't touch me. I need to know if you're going to touch me."

"Got it."

We walked towards the pool. She stopped a good ten feet from the edge and just stood facing the water. "I used to swim out here almost every day. I loved swimming."

"We can go swimming tomorrow if you'd like. I'll bring trunks."

She scoffed. "Like it matters what you wear or don't wear. I'm not going to see anything."

I smiled. "Maybe not, but there is still a line and I'm not going to cross it."

"Whatever. I'm tired. I want to go back inside."

She was lying. She wanted to get away from me. I recognized the retreat. "Why don't we sit out here for just a little bit?"

"Because I don't want to," she snapped. "I said I'm tired. I have a headache."

"I'll get you some Advil."

"I don't want you to get me anything! I just want to go back in!"

"Okay, got it. I'm going to grab your elbow and steer you back inside. Is that okay?"

"Fine."

We worked our way back into the house, following her directions to lead us to her room. I stood at the doorway and watched her go inside. The room was huge. Hell, I was pretty sure her bedroom was the size of my apartment.

"I'll be close by," I told her. "Holler if you need anything."

"Whatever," she mumbled.

I walked out and closed the door behind me, wondering if I had made the wrong decision.

Chapter Eleven

Bree

I COULD HEAR MALE VOICES and knew Luke had come back for another day. I thought for sure he would have quit and never come back after the way things went yesterday. When he had touched me, heat flooded my body. Like the best kind of electric shock. The little hairs stood up on the back of my neck and for a moment, I had forgotten I was blind.

It had terrified me. I didn't want to feel like that. I wasn't ready to think about being with a man again. Hell, everyone still thought I was still engaged to Nate. And, judging by how often he called and the texts he constantly sent, he still thought we were together as well. I had managed to avoid talking to him about anything serious, but I knew the talk was coming. I just wasn't ready to deal with it yet.

Following the voices, I made my way to the morning room. I could smell coffee, bacon and something sweet. "Good morning," I greeted them.

"Good morning, sweetheart," I heard my dad say. "I was just talking to Luke about your day yesterday. He said you guys spent some time by the pool and took a walk through the gardens."

"Yes," I said, not giving him any specifics about how short our time outside had been.

"I was thinking maybe we could go for a swim today," Luke said. He was close to me. I hadn't heard him move. "I brought my trunks."

A small smile spread over my lips. "Did you now?"

"I did."

"I think that sounds like a great idea. I've got to meet with my board today, but I should be home by three. Will you guys be okay?"

"We'll be fine, Dad."

He dropped a kiss on my forehead and left me alone with Luke once again.

"Can I get you some breakfast?" he asked.

I wanted to tell him no, but with my dad gone, it was either starve or let him help. He was being paid very well to help me, so I might as well. "Yes, please."

"Would you like to eat in here or outside?"

"Here is fine," I told him. I didn't want to risk stumbling and dumping food everywhere. It had happened once already.

"Great. Bacon?"

"Yes."

"Eggs?"

"No, never eggs," I told him.

He laughed, a sound I was really beginning to love. "Got it."

A minute later I heard the plate on the table in front of me. I felt around for the fork. I hated eating in front of anyone, since I made a bit of a mess.

"Can you give me a layout here?" I softly asked.

"Bacon at nine o'clock, toast at noon, and some fruit at three. Coffee is on your right."

I liked the way he said it. He didn't try and feed me. He just provided the information I needed to feed myself. "Thank you."

"Once you're finished eating, let's go out to the gardens. I know there is a lot more to explore."

I smiled, taking a bite of the bacon. "There is."

Together, we walked outside. I could feel him beside me. He never touched me, but his presence was enough to slowly guide me along where I needed to go. "Did you grow up in this house?" he asked.

"I did. I think we moved here when I was about four."

"It must have been pretty cool living in a house like this."

"I'm probably going to sound like a spoiled princess, but it was okay. My house was average compared to some of my friends."

He laughed. "I can't imagine this being average."

"I've lived a very privileged life."

He didn't say anything. I imagined he was thinking I was a spoiled brat, especially after the way things had gone down yesterday.

"There is a nice bench up ahead, facing a fountain. Do you want to take a seat?"

"Sure."

We sat down. I could hear the gentle flow of the water and smell the grass that had been freshly cut.

"It's very peaceful out here," he commented.

"It's a nice place to relax."

I noticed that when he talked, he was careful not to use seeing words. He commented about the way a place felt but never what it looked like. I appreciated that. It made me feel like part of the moment instead of a blind spectator sitting on the sidelines.

"What do you like to do for fun?" he asked.

I blew out a breath. "I used to surf a lot. I loved to paint. Anything outside, biking, swimming, hanging out at the beach."

"You use past-tense when you talk about what you like. Why?"

"Because that was my old life."

"Ah. I guess it's time you start thinking about your new life."

That hit a sour note. "There's nothing to think about. I'm blind. I can't paint. I can't surf."

"Look, I'm not going to pretend to know much about the non-seeing world, but I have treated plenty of patients that were visually impaired. One of them was a cook."

That was intriguing. "Really?"

"Really."

He had taken my snappy comment in stride. I reminded myself that he was getting paid to put up with me. "What about you? What did you do back in Texas?"

"The usual, roping calves, driving cattle, rodeo."

I couldn't see his face, but I could hear the sarcasm. I didn't need to see him to know he was teasing me. "Ha, ha."

"Sorry, I couldn't resist. Every time someone asks me where I'm from and I tell them, they all expect me to be a cowboy."

I grinned. "I get it. But for real, what do you like to do in your downtime?"

He was quiet. "I don't know. I never really had downtime."

That made me flinch. "Are you married? Kids?"

"No. Never been married. I'm out here by myself."

There was a lot I wanted to ask him, but I didn't want to pry. I liked my privacy and my secrets. He deserved to have his as well. "So, were you serious about going swimming?"

"Yeah. Are we going to do this?"

"Yep. I'll get changed."

We walked back inside and I dug out one of my bikinis, hoping it was a matching set. By the time I came out of my room, Luke was already waiting for me.

"Ready?" I asked, feeling a little self-conscience. I didn't know what he looked like beyond what Mel had told me, but I just had a feeling he was an attractive man.

"I'm ready," he said, his voice deeper than usual.

I wondered what he was wearing. Was he shirtless? Was he buff? When we got to the pool, I suddenly got cold feet. I hadn't gone swimming since the accident.

"I think I'll just get my feet wet," I murmured.

"I'm right here. We can do this."

He touched my arm and that flash of fire raced through my body again. "Don't," I snapped, jerking my arm away.

"Let's get in the water. If you don't like it once we're in, we'll get out."

"I don't need you to treat me like a child," I growled.

"Bree?" he said my name.

"What?" I snapped.

"You are about a foot from the edge of the pool. One hard shove and I will push you into the deep end."

I spun around, facing him with my jaw hanging. "What? You wouldn't dare!"

"I absolutely would. You won't drown, but it will take that attitude you're copping down a notch or two."

I couldn't believe he was talking to me like that. "How dare you! You're being paid to watch over me."

"I can swim. You won't drown."

Putting my hands on my hips, I was dangerously close to slapping him. Slapping at him, anyway. Instead, I shrugged off the cover-up I had put on, and very carefully inched forward until I felt the edge of the pool with my toes and then dove in, trusting I was at the deep end and trusting him to save me if I sank like a rock.

The moment my head went underwater, I let myself sink to the bottom. The water made me feel weightless. The feeling was amazing. I had forgotten how good it felt to be weightless in the water. A few seconds later, I felt a ripple in the water and knew he had jumped in.

I resurfaced, pushing the hair off my face and grinning wildly. It felt good—amazing even. I began to move, slicing through the water until my hand reached the edge.

"Left is the deep end," he called out from behind me.

Again, he was letting me do it on my own. I remembered what the rehab guy had told me about counting steps and committing it to memory to make my way around the house. It would be the same in the pool. I needed to learn how many strokes until I reached the end before turning and going the other way.

"Where are you?" I called out.

"On your right," he said, much closer than I expected him to be.

"I'm going to tie a bell around your neck. You keep sneaking up on me."

His soft laughter washed over me. "Just call me sneaky."

I splashed water in his general direction earning a splash right back in my face. "Hey!"

"You better get moving or I'm going to dunk you," he called out.

I burst into giggles before diving under the water and swimming away from him. I felt his hand touch my foot and moved faster. He was chasing me, which was probably not fair considering he could see me, but I couldn't see him. We spent some time racing back and forth in the pool.

"Ready to get out?" I asked him.

He chuckled. "I am. I have to tell you, I'm starving. Please tell me it's okay if we raid the fridge?"

I laughed again. "You do the raiding and I'll do the eating."

"Good plan. Follow the sound of my voice."

I did as he asked, following him to the edge of the pool. I climbed out on my own with no help. A fluffy towel was put in my hand. I took it and quickly toweled off before I was given the wrap. I led the way to the kitchen, perching on a bar stool as he rummaged through the refrigerator, calling out what he found and waiting for me to give him the yay or nay.

"Thanks for today," I told him when it was time for him to go.

"I didn't do anything. That was all you."

"Maybe it was, but I'm glad you got me in the water."

"Me too. I'll see you tomorrow."

I went back to my room feeling pretty good about the way the day had gone. It was nice hanging out with him. He was a part of the new life I was supposed to be creating. There was no link to my past with him. I didn't have to think about the things we used to do or how he used to treat me. There was no worrying about me not being the same person I was.

With Mel and my dad, I felt like I had to be my old self. But that person was gone. Trying to be her was exhausting. With Luke, I could relax. When I got snarky, he threatened to push me into the pool. Thinking about that sent me into another fit of laughter. I hoped my dad never watched the security footage. He would fire Luke, but not before he beat the shit out of him. Or tried to.

Chapter Twelve

Luke

IT HAD BEEN TWO WEEKS since my first day on the job with Bree. I had been worried about the emotional drain for nothing. While I knew she was still struggling with a lot of things, she internalized it. She had her moments and could get snappish, but it wasn't her real personality. I had spent enough time with her to know she was funny when she let go of that anger she had such a death grip on.

She was smart and witty. We had some long conversations about everything from the environment to her dream of wanting to open a gallery. We avoided the latter because it quickly sent her into a downward spiral.

I parked my car and headed inside the mansion. "Can we talk for a minute?" Paul asked, stepping out of the sitting room.

"Sure," I said, following him into the room.

"Have a seat."

I got the feeling I was in trouble. "What's going on?" I asked.

"I just wanted to check in and see how things were going."

"Good. Great. Has she said something else?"

He smiled. "No, not at all. I've noticed some positive changes in her. I'm happy with what I see. Has she talked anymore about her situation?"

"Her situation?" I questioned.

"Has she talked about getting better, getting her sight back?"

"No, not at all. Is that an option?"

He shrugged. "I don't know. I'm working on it. Don't say anything to her. It's not a subject she likes to talk about."

"I won't say anything. We're going to the beach today. Did she tell you?"

He smiled. "She did. I'm glad she's getting out of here. You're good for her."

"Thank you, sir."

"I've got to get going, but I just wanted to check in. Thank you for sticking it out. I know she can be a little difficult at times."

I smiled and got to my feet. "I like a challenge."

Heading for the dining room, I found her right where I usually found her waiting for me. "Hello Luke," she said, without me having to say a word.

"Hello, Bree."

"I poured you some coffee."

I looked down at the table and saw a cup of coffee waiting for me. "Did you use that new gadget?"

She giggled. "I did. It's pretty cool. It beeps to let me know when I'm getting close to the rim."

"I'm glad you're using it. Thank you for the coffee."

"I even added a couple sugars for you," she said, with a great deal of pride.

"Damn, you are one step away from being my wife."

She laughed. "Don't expect me to make dinner anytime soon."

"Your dad showed me all those gadgets he bought for you to use in the kitchen. They're pretty cool."

Her phone vibrated next to her, which was odd. I had grown used to one particular ringtone, a doorbell sound. She never answered the calls when I was around. I didn't question it and simply enjoyed the coffee.

"I'm not sure if I want to go to the beach. I don't think I'm ready."

"Bree, we've been talking about this for a week," I said.

"I said I'm not ready," she snapped, slapping a hand against the table.

Her temper tantrum moments were normal. I was used to them by now. "I don't care," I said. "We're going."

"No."

"Bree, I will drag your ass into my car and down to the beach."

Her head whipped around, facing me. I wished those beautiful blue eyes could see me. Her gaze was just over my shoulder. "I'm tired of you threatening me."

I smirked. "I'm not threatening you, sugar, I'm just telling you what will happen."

Her lips were in a thin line. It was the same push and pull we always went through. I waited to see how she would react. Sometimes she pushed, other times she gave in. "I'll go to the beach, but I'm not going in the water."

I smiled, knowing she couldn't see me. "Okay."

"I know that okay. You're still thinking I'm going to get in the water."

"I'm thinking you should wear your swimsuit."

She frowned. "You're such an ass."

"I know. Let's get a move on. Wear that sexy two-piece you wore in the pool the other day."

It was out before I realized I was saying it. I had no business flirting with her. She got up and took a step closer to me. "I'll think about it," she answered in a husky voice.

She was so close to me I could smell the coffee on her breath. Things had been getting very heated between us. We had never crossed the line, but there was no denying the pull between us. Being with her every day for the last two weeks had brought us close together. I felt like I knew her well. Too well. Like just then, I knew what she was thinking. Her lips had parted just a bit and her breathing had changed.

She stepped around me and headed for her room. I didn't have to follow her like I did in the beginning. She had grown more confident in her ability to navigate the area. I stepped into the bathroom and pulled on my swim trunks. I was going to get her in the water. Eventually, I would have her up on her surfboard. I had done some surfing when I was younger and hoped I could still stand up on the board.

I drove to the beach Austin had recommended. He told me it was out of the way and only a few locals used it. I didn't want to put her into a position that made her uncomfortable from the get-go.

"Ready?" I asked, taking her hand in mine.

She didn't flinch when I touched her anymore. Her hand gripped mine as we walked across the sand. "I'm not sure about this," she whispered.

"You're fine," I reassured her. "I've got you. I'm right here."

"Don't let go of me."

"I won't."

I spread the blanket out on the sand while she stood and faced the ocean. A gentle breeze moved her hair. She was wearing dark sunglasses, giving her the classic movie star look again. She had put on a black sleeveless dress that flowed around her body. I could see the strap of her black bikini and was looking forward to when the dress came off.

With all our time by the pool, she had regained the tan she apparently usually sported. She had asked me if she was tanning or burning. Then told me about how much time she spent outdoors before the accident. I liked learning about the woman she had been and the woman she was becoming now.

"Do you want to sit for a while?" I asked.

"Yes."

I helped her onto the blanket. We sat side by side, our shoulders almost touching. "This is nice," I commented.

"I've missed this," she whispered. "I know it's silly, but when I was little, my dad used to call me a mermaid. I even had a mermaid outfit. I spent so much time at the beach my nanny used to complain about it. So, my parents hired another nanny."

I laughed. "You were definitely not spoiled."

"I feel like the water gives me power somehow. Just being here has made me feel better than I've felt in a really long time. The sea calls to me. I feel the pull just like a mermaid would."

I looked at her and smiled, watching her take it all in. I was glad I had ignored her declaration that she didn't want to come. I knew she would like it once I got her to the beach. I didn't realize how much.

"Did you like the beach when you were younger?" she asked.

"I did. I didn't get to spend a lot of time at the beach though. It's what brought me out here. I wanted to experience the west coast."

"I'm glad you're here," she said.

I reached out to touch her hand. She grabbed it, holding it tightly in hers. It was very peaceful. Our relationship had evolved to the point that we could sit quietly together without needing words. I often found myself closing my eyes, trying to put myself into her world. I opened my senses, listening for the sounds she would pick up on.

"I think I like your Malibu," I told her.

She softly laughed. "I don't know if it's my Malibu, but I'm glad you like it."

"Want to get in the water?"

"I do. But don't let go of me."

"Not in a million years," I told her. I got to my feet and pulled off my shirt.

She stepped out of the dress and left it on the blanket before dropping her sunglasses to the blanket as well. I took her hand in mine and led her across the sand.

"I feel it," she breathed.

The water lapped over our feet. I stopped walking, letting her take the lead. She pulled me along as she waded into the water. She stopped when the water was just over her knees. "Good?" I asked.

She nodded. "I want to dive in. Can I?"

She wasn't asking me for permission. I squeezed her hand. "I'm right here. I won't let anything happen to you."

She chewed her bottom lip. "I want to."

"Do it, Bree. Just dive in. You're an excellent swimmer. I'll be right here. Listen for my voice."

She nodded. "Okay."

I released her hand and let her go. She slowly walked a little deeper into the water before her arms went up and she dove in. I proudly watched her, as if I was releasing a once injured animal back into the wild. She was my mermaid.

"Here," I called out when she resurfaced.

She turned around and walked towards me. The smile on her face would be something I always remembered. "Luke?"

"I'm right here," I said, and reached out to touch her waist with my hand.

"That was amazing," she whispered. "I cannot wait to tell my dad."

We spent another hour at the beach before I took her home. I made us a couple sandwiches before sitting down at the kitchen island with her.

"Next week, we'll have to drag out the surfboards," I told her.

She laughed. "We'll see." She took another bite of her sandwich before dropping it onto the plate. She turned to me. "Can I touch your face?"

"What?"

"I'm serious. I want to feel your face to get an idea of what you look like."

"Does that even work?" I asked.

"I don't know, but I think it might."

I wiped my mouth with a napkin and turned my chair to face her until our knees were touching. I grabbed her hand and brought it to my face. She put her hand against my cheek, brushing the pad of her thumb over my lips. I didn't move. Hell, I didn't breathe as her hand explored my face. The whole thing was incredibly intimate. Her hand pulled away from me.

"My turn," I whispered.

"But you can see me," she said with a small smile.

"I'm going to close my eyes. I want to feel what you're feeling."

"Okay."

I closed my eyes and put my hand to her face. I caressed the tip of my finger down her nose, touching her full lips. She sucked in a breath. My finger lingered as I brushed over her lips. I could practically feel what her lips would be like under my own.

My heart pounded in my chest and my own breathing came faster as the tension between us grew. With my eyes closed, there was no distraction. My other senses were heightened. I could smell the salty water on her. I could hear every inhaled breath, the short little gasps.

I desperately wanted to lean in and take the kiss she was offering.

"I have to go," I said, my eyes popping open as I jumped off the stool. "I'll see you tomorrow."

I walked out, heading for the door and not stopping. I couldn't kiss her. I couldn't get wrapped up with a client. She *was* a client. No matter how close we had become or how high the sexual tension was, the fact remained that she was a client.

Chapter Thirteen

Bree

I TOUCHED MY FINGERS to my lips. I couldn't believe I had almost kissed him. I couldn't believe I wanted to kiss him. The moment had been full of unspent passion. There was no way I could have been imagining it. I heard his breathing change. I swore I could even hear his heart thumping against the wall of his chest. I had found myself leaning into his hand. My wanton self damn near sucked on his finger. That would have been mortifying. Then again, he didn't kiss me, and I had been practically begging for it.

What the hell? I had been ready and willing, and he had walked away like I had reached out and bitch slapped him. I knew he wanted to kiss me. Why didn't he? I reached up and felt my face. I felt the thin line just along my hairline on my forehead. Mel and my dad had both assured me it was the only physical scar I had from the accident. I rubbed my fingers over my face and felt nothing more. I wasn't hideous—was I?

I slid off the stool on legs that were still shaking. The tension had been steadily building between us. I had felt it and knew he had too. It was impossible to deny. My skin felt hot and tingly, like we had just had a crazy make-out session. It had been nothing but the touching of faces, but it had felt like so much more. Touching his face, feeling the rigid jawline and the plump lips had given me an idea of what he might look like. I had felt the high cheekbones and the clean jawline.

It had taken all my willpower not to run my fingers through his hair. I could have said I wanted to know if he had short hair or not, but I had a feeling it would have sounded like the flimsy excuse that it was. It had been far too long since I had been kissed.

Being with him made me feel good again. I felt pretty. I felt alive. He touched me and I felt heat sizzle between us. His little reassurances here and there were subtle, but meant so much. He gave me strength and courage without even trying. All he had to do was say a couple words and the panic I felt evaporated. His breathing, his presence, everything about him was special. He was a balm to my very shattered soul.

I walked to my bedroom and immediately called Mel. I needed advice. I needed to figure out what the hell I was doing. I was in dangerous waters that I had no idea how to navigate. Even if I was my old self with complete sight, I had been out of the dating world for a long time. I needed insight.

"Hey," I said, when she answered the phone.

"Oh my goodness, you're actually calling me. I'm going to write this down."

"Ha, ha. What are you doing?"

"Um, watching Real Housewives."

I groaned. "Why do you watch that garbage?"

"Because when I grow up and get married to my rich husband, I want to know what not to do. These bitches are crazy."

I laughed. "Research. I get it. Come over why don't you."

"Okay, this is definitely a day of firsts. First you call me and now you invite me over. Are you sick?"

"Stop. I have to talk to you. Come over."

She let out a long sigh. "Fine. I'll be there in fifteen, but this better be good."

"I'll be in my room. Just let yourself in."

I hopped in the shower, turning the spray to lukewarm. I needed to cool off. I felt flushed. I was still struggling to understand what had happened between us. Technically, nothing happened, but it had almost happened, which was something. I heard a soft knock on my door and knew it was her. "Come in," I called out.

"Did you shut the door?" I asked her.

"Yes. Why?"

"Because I don't want my dad to overhear what I have to tell you."

"Ooh," she cooed. "This sounds juicy. I've missed our girl talk."

"So, I almost kissed Luke," I blurted out. I figured it was better to just come out with it then try to figure out how to explain it.

"What!" she shrieked. "No way. Did you do it? I would have done it."

"Shh, sit," I ordered, finding my way to the sitting area on one side of the room. "No, nothing happened."

"Tell me what *did* happen, and I know it's something or you wouldn't be freaking out."

"The last two weeks have been amazing. He's so patient. And kind. And we've really gotten to know each other very well. There is a tension between us. The chemistry is undeniable. It's weird to be attracted to someone you've never seen. I just feel this connection to him. I don't know if it's real or just because he's really the only other human I've had contact with besides you and my dad."

"I will vouch for his looks," she said. "He's hot. I would climb that man like a tree given the chance."

"I don't know if it's right though. Couldn't it be Stockholm syndrome or something?"

She giggled, and I heard her hand slap against her head. "That's when you've been kidnapped, you dork. He didn't kidnap you, did he?"

"No. Well, whatever it is, I'm wondering if I have formed an unhealthy attachment to him because he's my caregiver. What if what I feel isn't real? What if it's part of the trauma? The doctors said my brain was wired a little differently now."

"What do you feel?"

I groaned. "I don't know. Alive?"

"You are alive, dummy."

"You know what I mean," I growled. "Ever since the accident, I've been in this weird limbo. I wasn't living. I was existing. I've been so angry, I couldn't even smile. He has made me feel different. I feel like I am different. I don't feel like the old me, but like a reinvented version of the person I was."

"I think that's a good thing."

I blew out a long breath. "Is it though? Can it go anywhere? What if it's one-sided? What if he doesn't feel the way I do? This is his job after all. He's just doing his job."

"Girl, you are not an innocent. You know when a guy is hot for you. You don't need eyes to know that. If he's hot for you, he's hot for you. You said you felt it. Go with your gut."

I winced. "I'm scared."

"So, before I encourage you to go after your hot nurse, I think I have to ask about Nate."

Slowly, I shook my head. "You don't have to ask about him."

"I'm not sure what that means."

"It means Nate and I, well, I'm not worried about Nate."

"You guys having a rough time?" she gently asked. "You know he's probably struggling trying to deal with all this himself."

"He doesn't need to struggle."

"What aren't you telling me?" she asked.

"I'm telling you, I don't care what Nate thinks about me and Luke. It's none of his damn business."

"Rawr!"

I smiled. "Sorry. I don't want to talk about Nate."

"Got it, I heard you, loud and clear."

We chatted a little longer before she went home to finish watching her show. I stayed in my room the rest of the night. I was trying to sort through my feelings. I didn't know if my feelings were real or must an expected by-product of my situation.

I liked spending time with Luke. His quiet presence kept me from falling into that sinkhole that always left me feeling so alone. When I was by myself, I tended to focus only on my problems. I could make up even more problems just by letting myself think too hard. When I was alone, I thought about my old life. That never ended well.

When I was with Luke, I didn't think about all the things I didn't have or couldn't do. He was the doorway to a different future. It wasn't the future I had envisioned for myself, but it was a future. That was more than I had before I met him. I was getting too caught up, I warned myself.

I fell asleep that night thinking about him. I dreamed about what it would be like to kiss a man I had never seen. To do other things as well. Technically, sex was commonly done with the eyes closed, so being blind didn't change things too much. Except I wouldn't know what the man I was having sex with looked like. That was still a little strange.

I got dressed for the day, paying a little more attention to what I put on in anticipation of seeing Luke. I wished like hell I could put on makeup, but I wasn't feeling that brave just yet. My dad was already gone for the day, which meant it would just be me and Luke aside from the household staff.

I waited in the dining room for him. "Hi," I said with a smile when he came in.

"Good morning."

"I got your coffee for you."

He sat down in the chair next to mine. "Thank you."

"Are we doing the beach again today?"

"Bree, I need to talk to you about yesterday."

My heart did a little flip flop. "What about yesterday?" I asked, trying to sound casual.

"What happened, or almost happened, I'm sorry. It shouldn't have. I'm so sorry. I'll make sure it never happens again."

My heart sank. That was not what I expected to hear, or what I wanted. I had woken up that morning looking forward to seeing him again. I was hoping we could possibly explore what a relationship would be like between us.

Now, I felt like an idiot. Mel had repeatedly told me that he was a hot guy. Why would a hot guy want to date me? Even my fiancé, who wasn't really my fiancé anymore, didn't seem all that interested in a relationship. It was exactly as I had expected, I was damaged goods.

"I see," I said, once I had regained control of my sinking spirits. "I'm sorry if I gave you the wrong idea."

"It wasn't you. I think we can agree there's some chemistry between us. I don't want to do anything that makes you uncomfortable. I like working with you and I don't want anything to get in the way of that."

I pasted on a big, fake smile. "Good. I'm glad we can move forward. I don't think I'm up for another beach day. I would prefer to hang out around here."

"Works for me. Maybe we can do another workout in the gym?"

I didn't want to work out, but if I was on the spin bike, I wouldn't be touching him. "That sounds like a good plan. I love kicking your ass on the bike."

He chuckled. "I went easy on you the first time. I won't be quite so nice this time around."

The weirdness evaporated soon enough and I was looking forward to getting back to our normal way with each other. We headed for the gym but instead of his usual soft touches here and there, he kept his distance. Luke had gone from my enemy to forbidden fruit almost overnight. Maybe that was the problem. I couldn't have him, which was only fueling my desire for him.

Chapter Fourteen

Luke

I WALKED INTO THE HOUSE and could hear the very loud, angry conversation filtering down the massive hall. I followed the sounds of the arguing into one of the living rooms. Paul and Bree were at odds. My instinct was to go to her, to protect her. She was upset and I wanted to make her feel better.

"Should I give you guys some time alone?" I asked, interrupting the flow of the conversation.

Paul threw his hands in the air. "Maybe you can help me talk some sense into her."

"I don't need any sense talked into me!" Bree shouted back. "This is my life. Stop trying to control every detail."

I walked over to Bree and put my hand on her arm. "Let's sit down. What's going on?" I kept my voice quiet and calm, hoping to be the level head in the situation.

Paul sat down, his face ruddy and clearly irritated. Bree looked the same. Her cheeks were flushed, and she looked mad as hell. I waited, giving them both a few seconds to cool down. Whatever they were arguing about was serious. I had seen them have little squabbles in the past, but this felt serious. I could feel the hurt coming off of Bree in waves. Whatever was happening did more than just make her angry, it hurt her. I didn't like the idea of her being hurt.

"I've reached out to a new team of doctors," Paul began.

"After I told him to leave it alone," Bree interjected.

I put my hand on her bare knee and gave a gentle squeeze. "What kind of doctors?" I asked Paul.

"They are a team of specialists that work with traumatic brain injuries, especially those that have temporarily lost their sight."

"It isn't temporary, Dad!" Bree shouted.

Paul released a long breath, his eyes holding mine. "It could be. There is a chance they can reverse the blindness. They are using cutting edge technology and have had success with other candidates. It isn't a guarantee, but there is a chance. They are willing to review Bree's case and she refuses."

I turned to face Bree. "Why don't you want to see the doctors?" I asked.

"Because it's more false hope. It's more tests and empty promises and then it will end up being the same thing it always is. They'll tell me there is nothing they can do. I will have spent another couple weeks waiting and hoping only to be let down again. We've been down this road. I've seen several doctors and they all say the same thing. I don't want to go through the up and down of it all again."

I looked over to Paul again. "These doctors are different, Bree. They specialize in brain function and they have been able to successfully repair optic nerve damage in other patients. These guys aren't just neurologists or ophthalmologists."

In my mind, I couldn't see the harm in at least speaking with the doctors. I took a deep breath and turned to Bree again. "An appointment to hear what they have to say couldn't hurt," I said. "Maybe they can review the tests that have already been done to avoid putting you through any more."

"The doctor I spoke with said he would take a look at what the other doctors found. He was very hopeful that he would see something different."

"Stop talking about my life like I don't get a say in it!"

"Bree, it's one visit," I told her. "One discussion. Listen to what they have to say."

Her mouth was set in a hard line. "Easy for you both to say when you're not the one being used as a guinea pig."

"You aren't a guinea pig!" Paul snapped, his frustration bubbling over. "This is a chance for you to have your life back."

"I am never getting my old life back," Bree hissed. "It's gone. My sight is gone."

"One visit," I said again. "One discussion. If there is even the slightest chance for you to see again, how can you pass it up? If you are okay with your current situation, then you accept it and you move forward. There are days when you are so angry because you can't see and because you can't do some of the things you used to. What if you didn't have to have those days anymore? What if you could have your sight back?"

She slowly shook her head. "And what if I can't? What if they tell me it really is permanent?"

The emotion in her voice tugged at my heart. I suddenly understood. She did have hope. If she went to the doctors that were her last hope and they told her they couldn't help her, it was truly over. "If they can't help you, then it's time to embrace this thing and kick ass. You make the decision not to let the blindness stop you from doing what you want. You take back the control you've admitted you have lost."

Paul was staring at her. I could see her softening to the idea and hoped I had convinced her. I wanted the best for her. I knew she wanted to see again. I knew she was terrified to live in darkness for the rest of her days. This was her chance, possibly her only chance. I wanted her to take it, not because I saw her blindness as a problem, but because I knew it would make her happy.

"Fine," she said, her voice so low her father had to lean forward to hear. "I'll do it, but this is the last time. I can't keep doing this."

I looked to Paul to see if he agreed. I could tell he didn't want to make a promise like that, but he grudgingly nodded. I cocked my head to the side, reminding him she couldn't see his nod. "Okay. I will stop if this team says there is nothing left to do. Bree, you have to know I'm pushing because I love you. I will take you any which way you come, blind, seeing or whatever. I just want you to be happy."

The love he had for her was very evident in his face. I didn't have children, but I had seen the lengths a parent would go to in order to help their child. That bond was intensely strong, and I knew if Paul could do it, he would give her his own eyesight.

"Last time," Bree said again.

"I'll go make the call," Paul said, jumping up from the couch and walking out of the room.

I waited for Bree to say something. When she didn't, I figured she was waiting on me. "How do you feel about that?" I asked her.

"How do you think I feel? I'm being used as a guinea pig. I've been on this yo-yo for months and I'm so over it. He just won't let it go."

"I don't think he can let it go," I told her. "He is hurting right alongside you."

"I'm the one that can't see."

"Based on his expression, the pain in his eyes, he just wants to help you. Your dad strikes me as a powerful man, used to getting what he wants. I can't imagine how frustrating this must be for him. He can buy damn near anything, but all the money in the world is useless if he can't help his daughter."

She let out a sigh. "I know he cares, but I don't want him to get his hopes up either. It's killing him to see me like this and there is nothing I can do to change it. I've been trying to pretend everything is okay and that I'm the same person I was before the accident, but I'm not."

"He misses that person," I told her.

"So, do I."

"I think if there is even a tiny chance, you have to take it. I like you just the way you are, but I don't think you will be able to truly move on if you don't find out for yourself. Once you know one way or another, you take action. You decide what comes next. That's all on you. I will be here if you want me to be. If you get your sight back and want to kick me to the curb, so be it."

She smiled. "There are times when I want to kick you to the curb now."

I laughed. "Don't I know it! This may surprise you, Bree, but you don't always hide what you are thinking and feeling all that well."

Her bright smile warmed my heart. I cared about her more than I should. I was also pulling for her to get her sight back. I didn't want her to be able to see again because I thought it would make her more normal. I wanted her to see again so she could paint and do the things that brought her joy. I liked seeing her happy.

"What's the plan for today?" she asked.

"You tell me. Swimming?"

"I'm never going to turn down swimming," she said with a small laugh.

"Come on mermaid, your pool awaits."

We spent the day doing what we normally did. I almost felt guilty for getting paid to hang out with her. I made her lunch. We hung out by the pool, took a walk around the neighborhood and then listened to a few chapters of a book. It was like hanging out with a friend. Sometimes there would be moments where she would get frustrated or angry if she bumped into something or dropped food off her fork, but I just simply listened to her complaints.

I left for the day, making the drive to the small house I was renting on the property of an old lady who didn't need a caregiver, but liked the idea of having someone nearby. Austin had hooked me up with her. She was barely charging me anything for rent. I just checked in on her before and after work each day, which she seemed to love.

My phone rang. I glanced over, saw it was my mom, and figured I had better answer. It had been a couple days since I had spoken with her. I did miss her.

"Hi Mom," I answered.

"Luke! Finally! I was getting worried. I was preparing to call the police and file a missing person's report!"

"I'm just fine. I've been working a lot. How are you?" It was a loaded question and I knew what her answer would likely be. A litany of complaints about her back, feet, kidneys and who knew what else.

"I would be better if you were here," she answered. "I talked to that nurse you had come by. I'm not sure I like her."

"She's good people, Mom. Give her a chance. Have you been getting around okay?"

"Yes, I suppose, but it isn't the same without you here."

I sighed. "It will get better. I'm having a good time here. I love the weather and I'm getting used to the people."

"You could just come home," she said.

I smiled. It felt good to be wanted, but with her, it was dangerous. I couldn't let myself get sucked back into that toxic relationship. I was just now starting to feel like a normal person. I didn't want to lose the progress I had made. "I'm not ready to do that."

"Do you think you will ever be ready?" she asked.

"I don't know. I really like it here."

"Fine. What's this job you have?"

"I'm taking care of a young woman who was recently in an accident," I told her, not wanting to get into the specifics. I liked having a separate life, one that she wasn't wrapped up in.

"That sounds interesting," she said, without any real enthusiasm. "Is she crippled?"

"Mom," I groaned. She had zero tact. "She isn't crippled. She just needs some help here and there."

"I thought you were tired of caregiving?"

"It's a good paying job and I like it. It isn't a permanent job and I'm still hoping to get on at a clinic or hospital."

"I suppose," she murmured.

We talked a few more minutes before I ended the call. It was nice to be able to talk to her with distance between us. I couldn't get sucked into her drama from a thousand miles away. It was the start of what I hoped would be a healthy relationship for us.

Chapter Fifteen

Bree

I HAD NO IDEA WHAT Luke had up his sleeve, but I trusted him. He had shown up this morning saying he had a big surprise in store for me today. I had no idea what he was up to, but I was looking forward to getting out of the house and changing up our routine.

"Ready?" he asked, parking the car.

"I can't say if I am because you won't tell me where we are. I think this qualifies as abuse of the blind and I'm certain it is against the caregiver code."

He laughed. "I would never abuse you."

I heard him get out of the car and stayed put. A few seconds later, the passenger door opened, and his hand was on mine. He was old school. He always opened doors for me. I knew it wasn't just because of my blindness. He was just that kind of guy.

A cool breeze washed over me as I got out of the car. I could feel we were in the shade. "Where are we?" I asked, inhaling the air, trying to detect if we were near the water. I didn't hear the sound of crashing waves or the telltale signs of seagulls flying overhead.

"We are at a place I think you might like," he answered, taking my hand in his.

I heard birds chirping in the distance, along with hushed voices of various conversations. "Are we on a hiking trail? I'm not sure this is a good idea."

"We're not on a hiking trail, not yet. We are at a bird sanctuary."

I cocked my head to the side. "What is that?"

"It's a bird sanctuary, birds live here," he said dryly. "You know, for sanctuary."

I laughed. "What exactly are we doing here? Don't you come here to look at birds? That's kind of mean."

"Actually, no. A lot of birdwatchers never actually get to see the birds they are so desperate to watch. They blend in with their surroundings. But, birdwatchers also relish in the sound of the birds. That's what we're doing."

I slowly nodded. "Okay. I can understand that, but why? Isn't bird-watching for old people?"

His soft laugh washed over me. "I don't think there's an age requirement."

He held his hand in mine while he paid our entrance fees. It kind of felt like a date. I knew it wasn't a date. He was being paid to hang out with me, but it still felt nice to be treated like I was special. He led me down what felt like a brick pathway. He walked slow, alerting me to bumps in the path or when it turned left or right.

"Let's sit here," he said, gently pulling me to a stop. "It's a bench under some trees, which could be dangerous considering we're in a bird sanctuary."

I laughed. "I should have brought an umbrella."

"Listen," he whispered, squeezing my hand. "Do you hear them singing?"

I closed my eyes, a habit I wasn't about to break. I opened up my ears and inhaled. I imagined he was doing the same thing. He was completely still next to me. I could hear his steady breathing, feel the warmth of his body next to mine.

"Water?" I said the words as a question.

"There's a little pond with a waterfall not too far away."

I smiled. "Have you ever listened to those relaxation tapes?"

"No, but I've heard sound machines. A couple patients had them brought in."

"This is better than that. I can feel mist on my face."

He was silent as we both basked in the peaceful ambiance. We sat listening to the many different types of birds for what felt like forever. I could actually feel the strain of the last few months lifting. The longer I remained quiet, the better I felt.

"Should we go get some lunch?" he asked.

"I'd like that."

I felt truly happy. I couldn't remember feeling so at peace with myself in a long time. Even before the accident I had been antsy and on edge. It was nice to have a reprieve from it all. He took us through a drive thru before driving up the highway. He held my hand while I carried the bag of burgers and fries and he carried a blanket.

"Here should be good," he said.

I waited while he spread out the blanket. I sat down and waited for him to get set up. "Thank you," I said, when he put a burger in my hand. "This has been a really good day. Thank you for changing things up. You always seem to know just what I need."

"I try."

We ate in silence. For the first time since I had woken up from the coma and been told I was likely going to be blind for the rest of my life, I wasn't terrified of the future. He made me feel normal. I could see myself actually having a relationship, the kind that was healthy. Could it be? Could I actually begin to live again?

"I think I might be ready to try surfing again," I told him.

"That sounds like a great idea."

"Are you going to go in the water with me?"

"I will."

His tone was different. Something changed. "Luke, is everything okay? I'm at a bit of a disadvantage here. I can't see your face. I don't know if you're happy or sad. Take pity on a blind girl."

There was a soft chuckle. "I will not pity you. You are a strong, independent woman. You do not need to be pitied."

I popped out my bottom lip. "Sure, I do. I'm helpless."

"You are anything but helpless. I have no doubt in my mind you could kick my ass six ways to Sunday if you wanted to."

I grinned. "Possibly."

"Bree, I wanted to talk to you about something."

"What's up?" I asked, feeling lighthearted. Nothing could ruin my mood.

He cleared his throat. "I talked with your dad again," he started. "He said you changed your mind about seeing the specialist."

"I did."

"Why?"

"Because it isn't going to change anything. A whole parade of doctors told him my sight was gone. I don't understand why he won't listen. Why are you taking his side?"

"I'm not. I'm taking your side," he said.

I shook my head. "No. If you were, you wouldn't be sabotaging me like this. Is that why you did all this? You thought you'd butter me up and drag me out here and spring this on me?"

"I'm not springing anything on you. I just want you to do what's right for you. I want you to at least try. What's the worst that can happen? They say no?"

I jerked my hand out of his. "Exactly, that's the worst that can happen. Do you know what it's like to be given hope and then have it jerked away? It sucks. It builds you up and then you're dropped on your ass. I've done it too many times already. I don't want to do it again. I'm over it. You told me to accept my situation and move on. That's what I'm trying to do."

"But you're not," he shot back. "You're not moving on. You're stuck in this state of in between. You're angry and holding onto to the bitterness. You can't move forward if you don't let that go. You won't be able to truly move on until you've exhausted every avenue."

"I have exhausted every avenue! You don't understand. My dad is a wealthy man. People will tell him what he wants to hear for the right amount of money. They don't give a shit about me or what their bullshit lies do to me or my dad. They will string him along, take his money and then when they've milked him for all they can, they'll tell him they are sorry but there is nothing they can do. He's hurt. I'm hurt. It's serves no purpose to dish up false hope to anyone. They are preying on him and his pain."

"You don't know that for sure. He showed me the literature. It's a legit business."

I shook my head. "You don't get it."

"Get what?"

"You don't know what it's like to get your hopes up, bolstered by a bunch of bullshit only to have it yanked away from you. You don't know what it is to suffer from disappointment so big it absolutely crushes you."

"You don't anything about me," he hissed. "You have no idea what I do and do not know."

His words were full of anger and I immediately backed down. I had never heard him talk with such strong emotion in his voice. Our beautiful day was over. It had ended the moment he opened his mouth about the specialist.

"I'm ready to go," I said, anxious to get back to the comfort and safety of my bedroom.

"Bree, I'm not trying to piss you off, but this is important."

"I'm done Luke. I'm ready to go home."

I got up, dusting off my butt and waiting for him to lead the way. The ride home was tense. He tried to talk to me, but I was shut down. I felt betrayed. Like he had set me up, and I'd fallen for it like an idiot.

He and my dad had probably concocted their little plan to persuade me to go along with their idea of what was right for me.

The car came to a stop. "Are we here?" I asked, pissed that I didn't even know if we were home yet.

"We're here."

He got out of the car but instead of waiting for him to open the car door for me, I did it myself. I was already out of the car by the time he made his way around. "I don't need your help," I snapped when he tried to take my hand and lead me inside.

"Bree," he said with frustration. "I'm sorry you're pissed. I was only trying to help."

"Great. I don't need your help."

"I'll walk you inside. Your dad should be home soon."

I scoffed. "You don't need to walk me inside. I can do it on my own."

"I'm walking you inside," he growled.

He could be very assertive when he wanted to be. I stomped down the hall, heading for my bedroom with my chin high. I felt for the door handle and let myself in. I slammed the door behind me without saying a word.

He didn't bother trying to follow me in or say anything else. I flopped onto the bed, the depression I had been free of for so long back in full force. It pulled me back under the heavy cloak of anger and despair. I thought Luke was a friend. I reminded myself that he wasn't. He was a caregiver. He was being paid to be my friend from eight to five, five days a week. A friend didn't get paid to spend time with you.

I hated the tension between us and the feeling that I had lost a friend. I did believe he was sincerely trying to help. He just didn't understand how many times we had been given hope only to have it taken away. I had gone along for the ride every single time. I had hoped and prayed and waited and then been let down. Again.

I couldn't do it again. I didn't want to feel that kind of pain again. I had barely held myself together after the last time. There was nothing more to be done. Luke would just have to understand. If he couldn't then it was probably best if he found another job.

Chapter Sixteen

Luke

I WALKED BACK ACROSS the pathway that led between the guest-house where I was staying and the main house. My landlord was on her way out of town for the week. She was a sweet old lady, giving me free run of the backyard and the pool. I was planning on taking her up on the offer and going for a swim. First, I had to take care of some house-keeping chores.

It would be good to have some downtime. I hadn't slept well the night before and was looking forward to chilling out and doing nothing. Bree had thrown me for a bit of a loop the day before. I wasn't expecting her to get so angry. Maybe she was right, I didn't understand it. I had no idea what it was like to be blind. I didn't know what it was like to have something so important ripped away.

I flipped on Pandora and got busy cleaning up the house. When I heard a knock on the door, my first thought was that it was my landlord. I opened the door and blinked several times.

"Bree?" I asked with shock.

There was a blonde woman with her. I recognized her from the first day I had been at the mansion. "Hi," the woman said. "I'm Mel."

"Hi," I said, my eyes moving back to Bree. She was wearing her usual dark shades, her expression unreadable. "What's going on?"

"Can we talk?" Bree asked.

"Uh, sure. Here?"

"Yes," she answered.

"You good?" Mel asked her friend.

"I'll take care of her," I said, meaning every word.

Mel winked at me. "I know you will."

"I'll text you," Bree said.

"Come in," I said, a little weirded out by what was happening. I wasn't sure what she was doing at my house or how she even knew where I lived.

"Thanks," she murmured.

I put my hand on her elbow and guided her to the couch. "Can I get you something to drink?"

"No thanks."

I sat down beside her. "What's up?" I asked. "Is everything okay?"

"Everything is fine. I was just hoping we could talk."

"Sure," I said, a little nervous about what she wanted to talk about.

"Relax," she said with a soft smile.

"How do you know I'm not?"

"I can feel your tension. We've spent a lot of time together and I've learned how you breathe. I listen to your sighs. I know you."

I couldn't help but smile. "Way to use those heightened senses."

"I'm learning."

"Does your dad know you're here?" I asked, wondering if she had come to fire me.

"No. He thinks I'm out with Mel. When I told him I was going to spend the day with her, he was all too happy. He practically pushed me out of the house."

"He worries about you."

She sighed. "I know. You do as well."

"I do. I probably shouldn't, but I do."

She turned to face me. I let her leave the glasses on, but I wished I could see her whole face. "It's hard to be the source of worry for so many people."

"It's only because they care," I told her.

"I know. It's just, I've always been so independent. I've been the strong one. I only talked to my dad like once a week and now, it's like I'm a little girl again. He takes phone messages for me. Answers the door to announce visitors. I felt like I had to ask him if I could leave the house today. It's very strange to be stripped of all my independence. I'm not used to people worrying about me."

I chuckled. "I'm sure your dad has always worried about you. He just didn't show it like he is right now. Same with your friends."

"I don't like making them worry. If I could change things I would. I know my dad wants me to be whole again. He wants me to see those doctors because *he* needs me better. He doesn't want to worry about me."

I shrugged. "I think that's kind of obvious. He wants what's best for you."

"I know, but I don't think the false hope is best for me."

I wiped a hand over my face. I was reading between the lines. She was telling me what she didn't want. "I get it. You want me to mind my business."

She reached out. Her hand found my thigh. A very high spot on my thigh. I had to silently count to five. Her hand was making me think about things I had no business thinking about. "No, that isn't what I'm saying. I want to apologize for how I acted yesterday. I shouldn't have gotten so angry."

"I didn't mean to offend you or overstep. I'm sorry."

"Luke, I do value your opinion. I know you were trying to help."

"Bree, I am trying to help. You said you don't want the ups and down and I get it. I don't know your history. I don't know what exactly you've got going on in that pretty little head of yours, but I think if there's even a tiny chance you can get your sight back, you should take it. That's my opinion. I'm not in your shoes. I won't pressure you."

She turned her head, pulling her hand from my thigh. "When I talked to a doctor before, it wasn't long after I had come out of the coma, and he advised against any kind of surgery."

"Does your dad know that?"

"No. I am an adult and I asked him not to discuss it with my father."

I realized there was more to the story. I wasn't sure if I should press the matter. She had come all the way to my house, and I had a feeling she wanted to talk. "Why did the doctor advise against it?"

"Something about me dying," she muttered.

"Dying? What?"

"He said it was a risk. He said I could do the surgery and end up with brain damage or die. He said I needed to ask myself if being blind was worse than death. I told him to not talk to my dad about the options and to tell him it wasn't possible. Period. I was hoping it would get my dad to stop pressing me to get the surgery."

"But he went to another doctor," I said, finally understanding a little more.

"Yes."

"Why not tell him what the first doctor told you?"

"Because I don't want him to think about me dying. My dad can't lose me. I cannot die and leave him alone. He needs me."

I fought the urge to grab her hand. I wanted to comfort her. "I'm sure he went through a lot with the accident, but he's a strong guy."

"You don't understand," she breathed. "I'm all he has. I know if I died, he would not last long. We lost my mom when I was very young. I thought I was going to lose him. He didn't eat. He didn't sleep. He was a complete wreck. I saw him wasting away and was helpless to stop it. It wasn't until he hit rock bottom that he came back to me. I can't let him go through that again."

It gave me a little more insight into her hesitations. She was worried about her dad. I could certainly relate to that. "Bree, I really don't want to get in the middle of things, but can I give you a piece of advice?"

"Please," she quickly answered. "I would love to hear what you have to say."

"I think you need to talk to your dad, and tell him what that doctor told you. I have a feeling he wouldn't want to risk losing you either."

She worried her lower lip. "I know I should, but—"

I smiled, shaking my head. "But you don't want to tell him, because you're leaning towards the idea of getting the surgery, right? You're weighing the risk against the reward."

She blew out her cheeks. "I'm a mess. I know that. It's no wonder I have no friends left. No one can stand to be around my crazy ass."

"I don't think that's true," I assured her. "You're going through a period of change. We all go through them. Sometimes our lives change when we move to a new place, change jobs or breakup with someone. You're relatively young. There are going to be changes."

She smiled. "Are you sure you're not a therapist? It would be just like my dad to hire a shrink and try and pass him off as a caregiver."

"I am not a therapist but in my line of work, I do tend to talk my patients."

She wrinkled her nose. "I don't want to be your patient."

I laughed. "No nurse fantasies? You don't want to play doctor?" Once again, I said too much. "I'm sorry. That was inappropriate."

She giggled, pulling off her sunglasses. "It's fine. That's what I like about you. You treat me like a normal person. Everyone else is weird around me. Except for Mel. She is still Mel, but everyone else always felt so fake. Like they were afraid to laugh or joke around me. I felt like I was lying in a coffin rather than a hospital bed."

"I'm glad you don't mind the jokes, but I will try to keep it clean."

She threw up her hands, nearly hitting me in the face. "Don't! Just be normal. I'm not a little girl. If we were at a bar, hanging out and having fun, would you flirt and joke with me?"

"Yes. Absolutely." I would have been all over her if we had met in any other circumstance. Although, I would have hesitated a little. She was way out of my league. Her beauty would intimidate me had we met under any other circumstances.

"Then don't let the fact you're paid to hang out with me change anything. Just be you. I like being friends with you."

I smiled, knowing she couldn't see it, but I felt like smiling. "So, since you don't have to drive anywhere," I said, drawing out the words. "We can have a beer. I'm not on duty. I don't think we are breaking any rules."

She burst into laughter. "That's it! There's the silver lining!"

"What?"

"Mel is always telling me I have to look for the bright side in things, even this tragedy. I was not able to before, but hell, there is was right in front of me this whole time. I can get sloppy drunk and never feel guilty about not taking my turn as the designated driver! Yes!"

"Do you like beer? I guess you're probably used to something a bit more refined."

"A beer would be great. I love a cold beer while sitting on the beach and watch—"

I winced, feeling her pain. "You can feel," I said, moving back to sit beside her. "You can feel the sun moving lower, the air growing cooler. You can listen to the sounds that always seem louder when it's dark."

"I appreciate you saying that, but I don't think it's the same."

"I'll tell you what, we'll go down to the beach later on and watch the sunset. I'll tell you what's happening. I'll tell you what colors are flashing across the sky and whether the moon is full. I'll describe it all to you. You'll be able to see it in your mind."

There was a beautiful smile on her face. "I would like that."

"Good. Now, beers."

I got up and grabbed a couple of cold ones from the fridge. My house, rather my borrowed house, was nothing compared to her mansion. I wasn't sure what to do to entertain her. I didn't want her to leave.

I was looking forward to spending time with her without being paid to do it.

Chapter Seventeen

Bree

I TOOK THE OFFERED beer, letting the cold liquid run down my throat. It had been a while since I'd even tasted a beer. Once again, being with Luke made me feel normal. He gave me hope that there was a normal out there for me.

"What is this place?" I asked. I had gotten the address from my father's desk and Mel told it was a guest house, but I wondered how he found it if he was new to town.

"This is a guest house. I have a friend, well, I guess he's a friend. Anyway, he knows the lady that owns the place. I pay her a small rent and check in on her. She's elderly and in her house all alone."

"Ah, so you're stepping out on me," I teased.

His soft laugh from beside me sent shivers up and down my spine. "I would never step out on you," he answered in a husky voice. "She's gone for the weekend, the week actually."

"I see."

"I have the whole place to myself. Want to explore with me? I know there's a pool, but I haven't really looked around yet."

"Sure," I replied. "You can show me where you live."

"You probably would have fired me if you saw where I lived before. It was half a step above a hovel. I rented it sight unseen. When I showed up that first day, it was a bit of a shock. I had been sorely misled by the pictures I had seen. And it wasn't the best neighborhood, either."

"I'm glad you got out of there. We can't have any harm coming to you. Who would take care of me?"

"I'm not taking care of you," he whispered. "We're hanging out."

I smiled. It felt good to have him as a friend and that's what he was. I was glad I had made the spur of the moment move to come to his house. Mel had told me I was crazy, but I couldn't handle him being angry with me or vice versa. In a matter of weeks, he had become so much more than the guy that hung out at the house and made sure I didn't fall into the pool and drown.

"Let's do that exploring," I said.

He took my hand, holding it in his and led me outside. I carried my beer as we strolled around the grounds. I listened as he pointed out various objects and told me about the view, which sounded amazing. Then again, whenever he described anything, it sounded amazing.

"I have some steaks in the fridge," he said after a bit. "Wanna stay for dinner? I could grill them up and we can enjoy the sunset from right here."

"I would love that. I need to call Mel and let her know though."

He led me inside, giving me some privacy while I made the call from the small patio outside the guest house. "Hey," I said, in a low voice when she picked up.

"What's up?"

"I'm going to stay a while," I whispered.

"Like a while-while, or you're going to stay the night and finally climb that man?"

I giggled. "Stop. I don't know. Just a while. If I don't call you, assume I'm staying the night. If my dad calls you, tell him I'm with you. And I cannot believe I just said that. I sound like I'm sixteen."

"It's cool. I'll cover for you. Have fun, like really have some fun. He's a good guy. I knew it from the very moment I laid eyes on him. I am a little jealous, but I'll get over it."

"Thanks Mel. Talk to you later."

"All good?" Luke asked from somewhere nearby.

"All good."

We spent the next two hours, drinking beer and enjoying some very delicious steaks. I figured it had something to do with him being from Texas. I settled in on a lounger, knowing I was facing the water and the sunset, even if I couldn't see it, but I could feel it's warmth and for now, that was enough.

Luke was on my left, his hand holding mine from where he was stretched out in the other lounger he'd dragged close to mine. I loved touching him. He was my connection to the world. He made me feel like I was a part of the world I was in and not just a blob waiting in the shadows.

"Is it beautiful?" I asked him.

He squeezed my hand. "Not nearly as beautiful as you are."

I smiled, turning my head and trying to picture what he would look like beside me. "Thank you."

"For?"

"For being you. And for letting me be me."

I heard movement and a second later felt his other hand on my arm. "You're welcome. Thank you for letting me see who you really are."

He didn't speak for several seconds and I felt his fingertips sliding up my bare arm. I waited, somewhat helpless to do anything except wait.

"Luke?" I whispered his name.

I heard and felt the movement and then felt him standing over me. He gently pulled, indicating he wanted me to stand up. I was more than happy to do what he wanted. His hands slid over my waist, before moving back up. One hand cupped my cheek, holding me while his other rested on my hip. It was the moment I had been waiting for.

Though I could barely breathe, I stood with my face turned up towards his and hoped for the kiss I'd been longing for. It was a light touch, like butterfly wings. His lips brushed mine once, then again as if he wasn't sure he should. I was not going to miss my chance. I reached up, running my fingers through his short hair and pulled him in.

It was all the encouragement he needed. His mouth took mine, his tongue sweeping inside with a fiery passion I didn't expect. It was like a switch had been flipped. His arm slid around me, pulling my body close to his. I relished in the feeling of his hard strength. I heard a moan and realized it had come from me.

Luke's mouth pulled away from mine. "Oh shit," he breathed. "I'm so sorry."

I reached out, finding his shoulders and stepping close to him. "Don't you dare apologize! Kiss me, dammit."

"Woman, you have no idea what you're doing to me."

"I think I do. Take me inside."

There was a pause and then the next thing I knew his arm was behind my knees and he was lifting me. I shrieked, surprised by the feeling of floating through the air. His strong arms held me like I weighed nothing. A moment later I felt a soft bed below me as he gently put me down.

His body came over mine, his mouth ravishing my own. I hungrily kissed him back and it was better than I could have dreamed. I let go of all my inhibitions. Being unable to see him made the experience all the more erotic. My hands roamed his body until I found the hem of his shirt and tugged it up. My palms pressed against his broad chest, my fingertips digging into the muscle.

His shirt was pulled off. It wasn't long before my clothes were removed. I lay naked and wanting with wild abandon. Nothing else mattered in that moment. I was letting passion lead the way. His large, strong hand cupped my breast before his mouth came over my nipple. I cried out, arching my back and pushing my breast deeper into his mouth.

"Damn," he groaned. "You're so unbelievably hot."

He had no idea just how hot I was. I ached for him. "Touch me," I whispered.

His hand slid over my stomach, moving between my legs and stroking over my heated core. I groaned, my body writhing on the bed as he slowly made love to me with his finger. It had been too long since I had been touched. Too long since I'd felt such desire. My body was demanding release.

"Damn," he reverently breathed the word as his finger stroked inside me.

"Oh yes," I murmured, feeling the orgasm building. It was coming and coming fast.

When it broke over me, I was completely lost in the moment. My body arched and bucked, taking his finger deeper inside. He kissed me, his lips hard and demanding as my body wept with ecstasy. He was over me, his hot skin brushing over mine as he prepared to enter me. I ran my hands up and down his body, reaching down to take a handful of his ass in my grip. He was hard and firm all over.

"Are you sure?" he asked, his voice sounding strained, like he was trying to lift a car.

I responded by opening my legs and pulling him against me. He growled low in his throat, the head of his very large cock squeezing inside my opening. I winced, wiggling a bit to try and ease the penetration. I could feel him breathing hard and felt the strain in his arms as he held himself off me. He slowly pushed himself in deeper, my body stretching around him. There was a flash of pain and then my body suddenly opened to him.

I heard him release a hiss as his body fully engaged with mine. I took a few seconds to breathe deep, letting my body adjust to his heavy cock buried deep inside me. He began to move, our bodies doing a timeless dance as we chased after sweet ecstasy together. Being unable to see him above me wasn't so bad at all. I was able to notice all the other little things, like his breathing and the sound of our bodies sliding together.

It carried me away, taking me to sweet rapture. I rode the wave of ecstasy, surrendering myself to him and letting him lead the way to the climax I could feel waiting for me. In a heated flash of ecstasy, I heard him gasp, matching my own as he found his release. I nearly screamed as the force of his explosion inside me sent me to the highest peak I had ever experienced.

His body collapsed on mine, his breathing heavy and his heart nearly pounding out of his chest and into mine. I wrapped my arms around him, holding him close to me, pulling his weight down against my body.

"I'm squishing you," he murmured, moving off me a few inches.

I held him close. I liked the weight of him on me. It grounded me. It made me feel safe and protected from the darkness. "You're not. I'm okay."

"Are you really okay?" he asked.

I turned my face to his, rewarded with a soft kiss on my lips. "I am. I think I'm ready to see that new doctor. I'm terrified, but I'll do it."

"Do it for you, not for your dad."

"It will be for me."

"Are you afraid of the surgery or afraid of being told it isn't possible?" he asked, as his hand gently moved through my hair.

"Both. I'm afraid there will be a complication and I'll never wake up. I'm afraid of being told there is no way I will ever see again. I'm afraid of going through the surgery and waking up to discover it didn't work. I'm so afraid. I've never been so afraid in my life."

His strong arms pulled me against him. "I wish I could tell you not to be afraid. I wish I could take away the fear. All I can say is embrace the fear. Use it to fuel you. Once you own the fear, it has no power."

I let his words sink in. He was right, I was letting the fear rule my actions. That wasn't me. I was the girl who loved bungee jumping and the rush of adrenaline I got from doing new things. I couldn't let the accident change who I was at my very core.

"I will," I told him. "I'm going to do it."

Chapter Eighteen

Luke

IT HAD BEEN A LITTLE strange showing up to work that first day after our night together. I wasn't sure what to expect from her. I wasn't even entirely sure I still had a job. When I walked into the dining room, it had been just like every other morning. Breakfast was on the sideboard, Paul was reading the paper and Bree was drinking her morning coffee. Nothing had changed.

"Luke, do you have a minute?" Paul asked at the end of the day.

My stomach dropped. There was a very serious look on his face. "Sure."

He led me into his study and closed the door behind us. "Have a seat, please." I sat down and waited to be scolded or fired. "Bree has changed her mind about meeting the specialists. I have a feeling I have you to thank for that."

I smiled, shrugging a shoulder. "It was all her."

"Well, thank you all the same. I've made some calls and we have an appointment this week."

"Really? That soon?"

He winked. "Money talks in this town."

"She's lucky to have you fighting so hard for her."

"I would do anything for her," he said in a soft voice.

I nodded. "And she knows that. She's been worried about you as well."

"Me?" he asked with surprise.

"She's worried about you getting your hopes up. She doesn't want to disappoint you."

"She could never disappoint me. She's a fighter. I only want what's best for her. I want her to smile again. I want to hear her laugh again. Hell, I even want her to drive me mad with worry when she sets off on one of her overnight hikes or bungee jumping trips."

I laughed, imagining Bree living young and free. I wanted to see that for myself. My hopes were up for her.

Today was the big day. I was nervous and excited for her. I had shown up for work wearing a good pair of jeans and a button-up shirt. There would be no swimming or going to the beach today. The appointment was in an hour. We were all kind of killing time, waiting until it was time to go.

I looked around the living room, making sure Paul was nowhere to be found and stole a kiss. "Are you nervous?" I asked her.

"Terrified."

"It's going to be okay. You can always change your mind if you don't like what they have to say."

She blew out a breath. "I hate that I'm excited. I've been trying to tell myself to be realistic. I don't want to get my hopes crushed again. It's scary to hope."

"But you're brave and you're going to do it anyway."

I heard footsteps coming down the hall and moved away from Bree before her father walked in. "Bree, it's time to go," he announced. He looked at me, "Thank you for coming by today. We'll see you tomorrow."

In that moment, I felt like I had been slapped. Clearly, I was being dismissed. I had just assumed I would go with her to the appointment. I wiped my hands on my jeans and got to my feet. "I'll see you tomorrow," I said, and walked out of the room without saying another word.

"Goodbye Luke," Bree called out.

My heart hurt. I had been foolish to think I was more important to the family. I was the hired help. I wasn't her boyfriend. They had made me feel like part of the family and I had bought into the fantasy. It was easy to think the house was my domain. I had been given free reign, helping myself to the refrigerator, lounging by the pool and even borrowing books from the library.

But I was the help. Bree and I, that was hard to explain. I didn't know what was happening between us. We had the one night. We hadn't talked about what happened and aside from the occasional stolen kiss, there had been nothing more. The chemistry between us was still there, but it felt like some of the ache had been relieved. I still wanted her and would love the chance to be with her again, but before that happened, I needed to figure out what was happening between us.

I left the mansion and realized I had nowhere to go. I didn't want to go back to my place. I didn't want to sit and sulk. I had done a little exploring lately with Bree and knew there was a tiki style bar near my house. I was off for the day and felt like a few drinks were in order.

Changing into my usual khaki shorts, I pulled on my tennis shoes. I wasn't going anywhere that required me to be dressed any better than that. I strolled down the beach, surprised to see how busy it was in the middle of a workday.

"What can I get you?" an older bartender asked.

"Corona, please."

I paid him and took the bottle to one of the little tables on the edge of the beach. I watched the people milling about out on the sand. Mothers with bodies that looked untouched by pregnancy thanks to endless hours on spin bikes, access to personal chefs and the magic touch of a surgeon. Everyone was beautiful in Malibu. Even the kids were cute.

I watched as young couples lounged on blankets without a care in the world. I doubted they had jobs, and most were likely trust fund babies. They had nothing to worry about. They didn't have to find a job.

They didn't have to pay rent. They didn't have to take care of anyone. In fact, I was betting they were catered to and had servants to take care of whatever they wanted.

"Hi," a young woman said, pulling out the empty chair at my table.

I looked around and noticed there were plenty of other empty tables. "Hello," I said, slightly irritated by her forwardness.

"You're new," she said, pushing her sunglasses up.

She had the look of a Barbie doll. I couldn't tell if it was natural or fake. "Do you presume to know everyone in Malibu?"

A forced laugh followed by a very purposeful sip on her straw. It was meant to draw the eye to her lush red lips. I had seen plenty of lips enhanced by injections. They were pouty and perfect, and I imagined they could bring a great deal of pleasure to any man. "I do know everyone here. I've lived here forever and you're not from around here; that much I know."

I laughed. "I'm not from around here."

"You haven't recently bought property either, I would know that as well."

"Are you a stalker?" I teased, going along with her flirting.

She winked. "Only when I see something I'm interested in."

It would be easy. Too easy. "I'm not interesting. I'm a boring guy."

She made a big show of looking me up and down. "You're lying."

"Excuse me?"

"You're lying. You've got secrets. You're the kind of man that holds back until he either gets enough alcohol in him or finds the right woman to pluck at his strings until he releases his secrets. Among other things."

I raised an eyebrow, leaning forward. "I do have secrets. You should be more careful."

"Careful?"

Slowly, I nodded. "Careful. You don't know me or my secrets."

I stared at her long and hard until she leaned away from me. She pulled her glasses down before getting to her feet. "I think it's you who should be careful."

"Me? I'm just a guy enjoying a beer on a sunny afternoon."

"You're fresh meat," she snapped. "Ladies around here appreciate a new toy in town. They like to spice things up from time to time. I'm afraid once word gets out, you will be set upon by every woman under the age of fifty."

I smiled. "I'll keep that in mind."

She walked away, leaving me alone with my beer. She was an intimidating woman and I could see her as a legit man-eater. I would have to keep her warning in mind. I didn't dare allow myself to get drunk when I was at a Malibu bar. I didn't want to find myself in a position that would only lead to regrets.

Then again, I was single and in a new place. I should go out, explore the nightlife. I wasn't really the one-night kind of guy, but I was supposed to be starting over. I was supposed to be living the life I had missed out on. I had come to Los Angeles with the intention of living like I was a careless young man with nothing to lose.

But somehow, I just couldn't seem to shake the responsibility I felt. First, it was a responsibility to my mother. When my dad walked out, it had been me and my sister. Then my sister got out of town as fast as she could. I was the last man standing. My mother had made it very clear she couldn't live without me.

I had just rejected a very lucrative offer from a woman that promised to give me plenty of pleasure. I wasn't sure a normal guy would have done what I had done. I knew why I turned the woman down.

Bree.

"Fuck," I muttered under my breath.

I couldn't help but think I had jumped from the frying pan right into the fire. I had gone from one woman who needed me to another.

Bree was everything I said I didn't want to get mixed up in. I was a big softie. I couldn't turn down a woman in need. I would give and give and give until there was nothing left.

She could have stood up and told her father she wanted me to go with her. She didn't and it felt like a rejection. She needed me to make her feel normal, she said. I was essentially a pill. Like a medicine to help her forget her situation. I felt used.

I had no business feeling the way I did. I had been hired to do a job which I had done. Bree was using me as intended. I was happy I was able to help her through a difficult time. That's what I had set out to do. She was a broken young woman and I was proud of the little help I was able to give. I hoped it made a difference in her life.

Holding up my empty bottle, I grabbed the bartender's attention. A full replacement was brought to me almost immediately. I realized that I had probably talked myself right out of a job. If Bree did get the surgery and she regained her sight, there was no longer a need for my services and whatever I thought we had between us would be over.

"Easy come, easy go," I whispered the words my mother always said.

Maybe she had been right. Bree and I had hit it off almost immediately. We had developed a fast friendship. It had been too easy. And now it would slip away just as easily.

Chapter Nineteen

Bree

THE CAR PULLED TO A stop and the nerves in my belly took flight. I heard the door open and knew I was expected to get out. I couldn't get out of the car. My legs felt like jelly. I told myself it was no big deal. It was just a doctor appointment. I had been to them before the accident and would go to them again. I told myself it wasn't a big deal.

No big deal. Just my future depended on how the appointment went.

"Bree," my father's voice came from my right.

"I can do it," I said getting out of the car.

He hooked his arm through mine. I heard a siren in the distance, growing closer by the second. In a flash, I was back in my smashed car, blood dripping into my eyes. Darkness engulfing me as terror raced through my veins.

I stumbled, snapping myself back to reality. "Bree are you okay?" My father's voice cut through the fear clouding my brain.

"I'm fine," I snapped.

The siren grew louder, coming closer, just like that night. I still awoke to the sound of a screaming siren in my head. I remembered the sirens and the voices of strangers telling me to hold on. Then there had been the horrid grinding sound as the firemen had cut through the metal of my car. I knew I had faded in and out of consciousness. It felt like I had been trapped in the car forever. I remembered asking them over and over to turn on some lights.

My heart was pounding fast in my chest. Too fast. I knew what was happening. It was the onset of another panic attack. "Take a deep breath," my father's voice came through loud and clear.

I tried. I grew angry because I couldn't. "Let go of me," I shouted.

"Bree stop it."

I yanked my arm away from him. And blindly walked forward. I had no idea where I was going. I probably looked ridiculously with my arms extended as I felt for anything that might get in my way. My father's strong arm wrapped around my shoulder. "Stop running."

"I'm not running. I want to go home."

"We have an appointment!"

"You didn't tell me it was at a hospital," I wailed.

I felt the whoosh of doors sliding open and was suddenly assaulted by the sound of a voice calling out for a doctor. Again, I was transported back to the hours following my accident. The incessant beeping and the paging over the intercom had sounded a hundred times louder.

"Of course, it's at the hospital," he snapped irritably.

"I don't want to go inside," I whispered.

"You are inside."

"I want to go," I said the words on a breath.

"We have an appointment. Let's go."

I violently shook my head. "No. I can't. I want to go home."

He dragged me along, taking me away from the hustle and bustle. I was making a scene. I knew it and I didn't care. "Do your breathing exercises," he said in a quiet voice. "You can work through this."

"No! Let me go. I want to go home. Please."

"Take a deep breath," he ordered.

I felt like I was going to throw up. My head started to spin. I clapped a hand over my mouth, my other hand reaching out for something to ground me. I needed a wall. I needed Luke. He always had such a calming effect on me. He could talk me down from a panic attack just by touching my hand or the spot on my lower back.

"I want to go," I shouted, on the verge of hysteria.

"Shh," he scolded, taking my hand and dragging me somewhere. "Just calm down. Relax. You're okay. I'm right here."

I heard an elevator ding. I pulled back, yanking my hand out of his once again. "No! I cannot go on the elevator!"

The thought of going into an elevator and being sealed in a box only served to heighten my panic. I clawed at my father when he tried to touch me. I couldn't handle being touched. I was in a sensory overload and needed to escape. I turned, my arms stretched out in front of me as I walked through the hall.

"Gabrielle," my father shouted behind me.

I kept moving. I could feel the fresh air, hear the doors sliding open and knew I was close. His arm was around me once again. Instead of trying to stop me, he guided me back outside. The fresh air helped, but I still couldn't quite catch my breath. My chest felt tight enough I feared I was having an actual heart attack. I remembered the doctors telling me it was the anxiety and I would be fine. I just had to ride it out. I was trying, but I couldn't see a light at the end of the tunnel—literally.

"Sit down, there's a bench," he said.

I sat down and bent forward, trying to suck air into my starving lungs. His hand patted my back. It wasn't comforting. It only antagonized the panic. I leaned away. "Don't."

"This is unnecessary," my father hissed.

I didn't answer. I couldn't speak. I took several deep breaths and focused on my breathing. I tried my hardest to get the panic under control. Slowly, I could feel my breathing slowing. The dizziness subsided and I began to feel almost normal.

"I'm sorry," I said, feeling absolutely ashamed of myself.

"It's okay, take a minute and we'll head in. We were early anyway."

I slowly shook my head. I realized it had been a mistake to agree to the appointment. "I'm sorry. I can't do it. I can't go in there."

"Sweetie, you can. I know it's tough. But it's just going to take some gumption. You can do it."

"No, Dad. I don't want to. I need you to listen to me. I'm sorry I wasted your time. I shouldn't have. You can tell them it was all me. Tell them I panicked. I don't care what you say. I'm not interested in talking about it anymore. Just take me home."

"You are not a quitter," he said firmly.

I hated letting him down. "If you won't take me home, I'll call Mel to pick me up."

"Dammit Gabrielle! We've come all this way. We're steps away from getting you some help. You can't stop now!"

"It isn't help dad! It's more bullshit. More people willing to take your money and blow smoke up your ass."

I heard him gasp. "Keep your voice down. You're embarrassing me."

"I don't care. You put me in this position. Take me home and I won't embarrass you anymore. I'm so sorry to have made a scene. Trust me, I would love to storm out of here and leave you alone, but I can't. I'm stuck. Don't make me beg. This is bad enough."

"All I'm asking is for ten minutes. Give the doctors ten minutes."

I jumped up from the bench. I was desperate and he wasn't hearing me. I stepped forward, bumping into someone. I quickly apologized and stepped forward again.

"Dammit, Bree. Stop!"

I ignored him. I knew I was walking headlong into a parking lot and could be run over at any second. I couldn't seem to care. My father's hand roughly grabbed my arm, stopping my progress.

"Let me go," I sobbed.

He didn't release me. His grip tightened as he dragged me in a different direction. "We're going to the car. Quit struggling. Someone has probably called the police already. We're almost to the car."

"You should have let me go," I whispered. "I don't want to be here."

The car door was opened. I felt my way inside, putting on my seatbelt while I waited for my dad to get in. I was on the verge of hysteria. I was barely holding it together. Who was I kidding? I wasn't holding it together at all.

The car started and I felt it move. I tried to calm myself. We were going home. I did the counting exercises the therapist had taught me. I tried to slow my breathing. Every time I thought I was getting over it, a new wave of panic washed over me.

"I'll call and reschedule," he said, and I could hear the anger and frustration in his tone. I felt like I was sixteen and he had just pulled me out of a wild party. He was angry and disappointed in me. I hated letting him down. Between the panic and the feelings of being inadequate, I couldn't remember a time when I had felt more miserable.

The drive home was quiet. I could feel the anger coming off him in waves. I loved him. I absolutely loved him, but in that moment, I was not happy with him. I wanted him to understand why. I wanted to tell him how I felt. I couldn't find the words. I wanted to tell him I was struggling. I wanted to tell him I was barely holding on.

"We're home," he announced in a tight voice. "We're in the garage."

"Thank you," I muttered, appreciating his information.

I got out of the car and very slowly made my way around the front. He reached out and touched my arm. I jerked away.

"Bree stop being so stubborn."

"First you're pissed that I'm not fighting hard enough, now you're pissed that I'm too stubborn."

He let out a long, frustrated sigh. "I'm not pissed. I just don't understand why you won't do what is necessary to help yourself. Do you like being the way you are?"

I gasped as if I had been slapped. I spun around, knowing he was somewhere in the general area. "Exactly what would that be? Blind? Stubborn? Broken?"

"You're hysterical," he snapped.

I turned around and walked towards the door I knew wasn't too far away. I didn't stomp my feet, but I wanted to. I kept moving, knowing my bedroom wasn't far. I was so close. I made it to the door and let myself in. I slammed it behind me. Taking great pleasure in hearing the hinges rattle. I couldn't have a proper tantrum without being able to see where I was running away to.

I threw the lock and kicked off my shoes as I walked across my room. I fell face first on my bed and released the tears I had been holding back. I hated that I had let him down. It wasn't just my father that was disappointed. Luke would be upset as well.

"What are you doing Bree? You have to pull yourself together."

I wavered between wanting to stand up and scream 'I am woman, hear me roar.' I wanted to embrace the blindness and be one of those prodigies that became an internet sensation. I wanted to be a blind painter, creating masterpieces.

Then there was that other part of me that said, 'give up.' That little devil on my shoulder told me it was okay to wallow and cry. That I deserved to be angry and could lash out at anyone around me. I felt like I was being ripped apart. The inner war happening inside me was killing me. It was toxic energy eating me up.

I had to make a decision. I could choose to live or choose to die, because the dark world would kill me. I cried until I had no more tears left to cry. The crying jag had exhausted me, leaving me completely drained. I crawled under the blanket and closed my eyes, praying for blissful sleep.

Luke, rather the image I had conjured in my mind of him, floated through my mind. I felt his warm hands on me. I could hear his soft laughter. I let the fantasy of him shift gears and thought about the way it felt to have him inside me. I remembered the first gentle kiss and smiled. He'd been tender and sweet—until he wasn't.

I sighed with the memory of him and wondered if he would ever want me now that he knew there was no chance I would ever get my sight back.

Chapter Twenty

Luke

WHEN I WALKED THROUGH the front door of the mansion, I immediately felt the negative energy. I wasn't sure why, but I practically tiptoed through the foyer. I walked to the dining room and found it empty. My first thought was that Bree was in the hospital. That she had gone forward with the surgery already. I didn't know if it was something that was even possible, but I hoped.

I walked back down the hall, wondering if I should knock on the door to her room or let myself out.

"Luke," Paul's voice boomed down the hall.

Spinning around, I saw him waving me into his study. I had learned that was his private domain and only the most serious conversations took place in there. My stomach twisted into knots as I walked towards him. I had no idea what was wrong, but it was clear by his dour expression and the chill in the air that something was.

"What's up?" I asked, trying to keep it casual.

"Have a seat," he grumped.

The door closed behind me. *He knew.* He knew about me and his daughter. I wasn't sure if he would simply fire me or if he would do what he could to ruin my reputation. I had known it was dangerous. Known it was a mistake to have sex with her, but it had been one of those moments when I decided to ask for forgiveness rather than permission. Staring into his eyes filled with what looked like anger made me rethink that decision.

"What's going on?" I asked, my voice an octave higher than usual. "Did the appointment go well?"

"We didn't make it to the appointment," he said, and I could see the irritation on his face.

"What happened?"

"She had a panic attack. I'm afraid she hasn't quite recovered."

I leaned forward. "What do you mean? Is she alright? Is she here?"

"She's in her room. She won't come out."

I wanted to jump out of my chair and rush towards her. I held fast. "I see."

"I'm hoping you can bring her out of this. I haven't seen her this bad since she first came out of her coma. It scares me to see her like that."

I nodded. Neither of them talked much about the accident or the time she was in the hospital. I didn't pry. I knew it was traumatic. They would talk when they were ready.

"I'll do what I can," I said, anxious to get to her.

"I'll be out of the house most of the day, which I'm sure will make her happy. I'm not exactly her favorite person right now."

I offered him a smile. "I'll work with her. She loves the beach. I'll try and get her in the water. That usually cheers her up."

"Good. Do that. I'll check in with you later."

Jumping up, I left the study, heading towards her room with no idea what to expect. I had seen her have a minor panic attack, but this seemed different. Her dad had made it sound very grim. I knocked on the door to her room. She didn't answer.

"Bree, it's me," I called out. "Can I come in?"

"No," she answered.

I smiled. At least she answered. "Bree, I'm coming in."

"Go away."

"I can't," I said, and turned the door handle. It wasn't locked, which told me she wasn't all that serious about keeping me out. We'd had arguments in the past and she had actually locked me out.

She was sitting in her favorite chair that had been dragged close to the window. "I said go away."

Closing the door behind me, I walked over to grab the other chair. I dragged it over and sat down. "I don't want to go away."

"Has anyone ever mentioned you can be a royal pain in the ass?"

"More times than I care to count."

"Did he tell you?"

"Did you want him to?" I gently asked.

"I don't care, but I don't want to talk about it."

"Works for me. Want to go swimming?"

"No. I want to be alone."

I could see she was in pain. I wanted to make it better, but I also knew she wasn't the type to want to talk about what she was feeling. "Okay. We'll just be alone together."

She turned her face to mine. Her hair was piled on top of her head in a messy hairdo that actually looked very stylish. Her eyes had dark circles under them and I could see the evidence of what must have been a very long, sad night.

We sat together, not talking. I listened to her breathing, doing my own assessment about how she was doing with my ears. I felt like I knew her so well, I could sense when she was happy, sad or scared. When I had come into the room, her anger and frustration had been apparent. I could feel her calming and knew my presence was helping. I was doing all I could do for her.

Her bedroom door suddenly opened, startling the both of us. I expected it to be Paul or the housekeeper. It was neither.

"Who are you?" the guy asked.

I got out of the chair and stood between him and Bree. "I'm Luke, who are you?"

"Bree?" the guy said.

"Nate?" she got to her feet, her hand touching my back before she stepped around me.

"Your dad said you were in here with your caregiver," Nate said, his eyes locked with mine.

He didn't look happy. I knew a jealous boyfriend when I saw one. He was definitely jealous and didn't like me, judging by the way he was sizing me up and down. I smirked, knowing I was taller and bigger than him. He had a bit of a rich boy 'Slick Rick' kind of thing going on. I wanted to punch him on principle.

"Luke, can you give us a minute?" she asked.

Turning to look at her, I wasn't exactly thrilled to be kicked out of the room. I reminded myself I was her employee, not her boyfriend. Apparently, that spot was already filled. "I'll be right outside," I told her, my eyes locked on his.

I touched her arm out of spite. Letting him know she was comfortable with my touch. It was a dick move meant to incite his jealousy. I wanted him to feel the same jealousy I felt. I had no reason to be possessive, but I was.

"Close the door on your way out," Nate snapped.

I almost hit him. I wanted to slap the smug look off his face. I closed it, leaving it open a crack. I didn't trust the guy. Bree had not looked all that thrilled that he was here either. I leaned against the wall outside her bedroom, ready to rip the guy to shreds if I heard her call for help.

While I waited, I thought back to the ignored calls. It had been him. I knew it. I had a feeling she had been hiding something from me, but I had never though it was a boyfriend. I'd never heard her talk about a boyfriend. I had made myself believe there wasn't a one.

Paul happened to walk by, pausing when he saw me outside the room. "Did Nate find you guys?"

I nodded. "He did. He's in there now."

"Ah good. The poor boy has been trying to catch up with her for weeks."

Offering a tight smile, I replied, "He found her."

No sooner had I finished my sentence when the door swung open and Nate stepped out. He shot me a glare before he saw Paul standing in the hall as well.

"How did it go?" Paul asked.

I watched his face transform into a pitiful, dejected man. "She's asked me to leave. I'm trying Mr. Sullivan, I swear I'm trying. It's killing me to see her hurting. I don't know what to do."

Paul stepped forward and patted the guy on his shoulders. "She'll come around. She had a rough day yesterday. Just give her some time."

Anger raced through my veins. I watched as Paul walked Nate to the door. The two of them looked like old friends. That gave me the idea they had known each other a while. Bree's bedroom door stood open. I debated whether or not to go in and check on her or leave her be.

"Did he leave?" she asked standing in the doorway.

"He did."

"Thank goodness. I'm starving."

I took a deep breath and reminded myself I was there to look after her. I couldn't get upset about her having a boyfriend. "I'll make you something to eat."

We walked to the kitchen. She sat down while I grabbed the stuff needed to make her a sandwich.

"Bree," Paul said coming into the kitchen. "What is going on with you guys? He's been calling and stopping by all this time, and I'm pretty sure he's bought out half the flower shops in Malibu."

I pretended not to hear anything. My back was to them as I spread mayonnaise on the nine-grain bread she liked.

"Dad, I am not talking about that with you," she mumbled. I figured she was trying to keep me from overhearing them talk about her boyfriend.

"He's a good man. You two have been together a long time. He's good for you. I know you are having a rough time but think about what he's feeling. This can't be easy on him either."

"Gee, I'm sorry my blindness is upsetting him," she snapped.

"I'm only saying he was absolutely crushed when he got to the hospital. He was so worried about you. He stayed by your side quite often while you were in the coma."

"I don't care. This is between me and Nate. I'm not talking about it with you."

"Don't be like that," Paul cajoled. "You used to talk to me about your life all the time."

"Not this and not now."

I cut the sandwich in half and slid it on a plate. "Here you go," I said, trying to sound totally casual about the whole thing.

"Thank you."

Paul sat down on the stool next to his daughter. "I think you need to talk to him. At least tell him you need some time. Don't shut him out."

"I have talked to him," she said, through gritted teeth. "He isn't listening. That's something the two of you have in common. Leave it alone. Please."

Paul sighed and looked like he was going to say more. "Can I make you a sandwich?" I asked before he could say anything more to Bree.

"Um, yes, please and then I do have to get to the office."

Turning away, I started making a second sandwich. It gave me something to do with my hands. I didn't know why I was trying to help her. She had betrayed me in the worst way. I was beyond furious. I wasn't even that mad that she had used me for sex, but I was pissed she had a boyfriend waiting in the wings. She had played me for a fool.

I wasn't sure if she had done it on purpose in an effort to make the boyfriend jealous or if she was trying to make me jealous.

Either way, it was scandalous. It was making rethink everything I thought I knew about her. I had to wonder how long she'd been playing me. Was she even who she seemed to be? She acted like the injured victim, but I had seen that stronger, kickass side on occasion. Had she been playing up the wounded girl to pull at my heartstrings?

It was all very reminiscent of my mother. I could not let myself get into a mess like that again. I could not be used and toyed with like my feelings didn't matter. Like I didn't matter.

I handed the sandwich to Paul. "Here you go."

"Thanks, Luke. I'll be home late. Are you able to stay a little later than usual? The housekeeper can't stay, and I don't want Bree alone."

"I'm not a child!"

"Yes, I can stay," I answered, ignoring her latest tantrum. I was in no mood to hear her opinion on much of anything.

Bree had the nerve to look pissed. It only infuriated me further.

Chapter Twenty-One

Bree

I HEARD MY FATHER WALK away, leaving Luke and I alone in the kitchen. I took a bite of the sandwich. I had skipped dinner and breakfast and I was starving. I was happy to have Luke there. I wasn't sure I was ready to talk to him about what happened with the doctor appointment. Not yet.

"Juice?" he asked. It wasn't a polite question. He was obviously pissed.

"Yes, please," I answered.

I heard the glass clink against the hard counter. Then it was the gurgling sound of juice being poured into the glass. "Here. On your right."

Someone had woken up on the wrong side of the bed. I finished eating and waited for him to ask me to go sit by the pool again. I could hear him in the kitchen, but he wasn't speaking, which was a little strange. "Maybe we can sit in the solarium?" I asked.

"Sure."

Clearly, he was pissed. "Is everything okay?" I asked feeling his hand touch my elbow.

"Yep. Right as rain."

That was bullshit. "I'm glad you're here."

"Sure," he said, his voice tight.

I could feel the tension in him as we made our way to the solarium. I wasn't sure what had been said between him and my father while I had

145

been in my room, but I was going to find out. He helped me settle into a chair before taking his own seat. He wasn't next to me. I could feel it. That wasn't normal.

"So, who is Nate?" he asked, after a very long, tense silence.

Part of me wanted to smile. That is what had him upset. Another part of me didn't want to talk about Nate. Nate was the source of some pretty bad memories. He had already barged in and brought up the night of the accident. I shouldn't blame Nate, but I did.

"Nate is a complicated story," I answered.

"You didn't tell me you had a boyfriend. A serious boyfriend by the sound of it."

I scoffed. "Fiancé actually."

"Wow," he said, his voice flat. "I guess I should have asked more questions."

"It isn't like that," I told him hearing the anger in his voice.

"It certainly, seems that way. I didn't know. I do now. Seems like you might have mentioned it."

"Luke, you don't understand." Memories from that night flashed through my mind. I thought about the fight and how angry I had been. I had jumped in my car and sped away. I had been going fast. I had been furious with Nate. Years of putting up with his bullshit had culminated that night. Headlights flashing in my eyes before everything went dark. That was how I would always remember Nate.

"Why don't you help me understand?" he growled. "Your dad is pretty sure the guy walks on water. You've had a boyfriend, I'm sorry, a fiancé this whole time and you made sure to never mention him. I don't like to play games, Bree. I'm not here for you to fuck around with and use. If you need a buddy, maybe you should call Nate."

I shook my head. "No! I will not call Nate. I don't want him around me. I've ignored him because I have nothing to say to him."

"Why?" he asked. His voice was closer. He had moved next to me.

I had been carrying the burden of what happened that night for too long. I had given Mel cliff notes, but hadn't been able to tell her the whole story. I needed to tell Luke.

"We broke up," I whispered.

Luke made a sound. "I don't know any guys that continually call, text and send their ex flowers. So all that's been him all this time, right?"

I slowly nodded. "It is, but I don't want to talk to him. I've told him that and he doesn't seem to get it."

"Why?" he asked. "Why don't you want to talk to him?"

The flashbacks came faster, angry snippets of our conversation that night. When I had opened my eyes in the hospital and learned my fate, I had been furious. Furious with Nate. I had not been able to let that anger go. It was white-hot, burning through me and settling in my stomach.

"We broke up," I confessed. "We broke up that night, right before the accident. We had gotten in a fight. Again. We were always fighting. He was always hounding me about the wedding. I didn't want to get married. I told him over and over I wanted to wait. He said some nasty things and I got pissed. I ended it with him. I told him we were not getting married. I stormed out of the apartment, got in my car and drove off like a bat out of hell. I was so mad. It was raining hard which only fueled my anger. I had the radio up loud, trying to drown it all out."

"Ah," he said softly.

I reached out to him. His hand found mine. "I saw the truck coming towards me and I had nowhere to go. It was on me before I had a chance to do anything."

"It was the other driver's fault," he assured me. "I was told he was cited for going too fast for the conditions."

I shrugged. "I was driving too fast as well. The difference is I was in my car and he was in his big ass truck. Semi one, BMW zero." I sighed.

My last vision was the one thing I wish I could erase. "Nate just assumes he can walk back into my life like nothing happened."

"Why does your dad think you two are still together?"

"Because I haven't told him. I didn't want to tell him I had been driving pissed off that night. It's just more drama. Plus, I don't know if you noticed, but my dad likes Nate. They are buddies. It's why I waited so long to break up with him. I didn't want to disappoint my dad. I kept thinking we were going through a phase and I would eventually get over it. But I didn't. Things just kept getting worse and that night, it all just came to a head."

"Bree, I'm not sure what to say. Did you tell Nate how you felt today?"

"I did. I told him it was over, but like always, he thinks I'm just being silly and once I get my sight back, things will be okay. I'm sure he and my father have discussed the matter. It pisses me off. I'm sick of being treated like a child. The two of them are convinced I don't know what's best for me and they've been trying to control me for years. I'm done with that. I don't want Nate."

"I see."

"Were you upset because you thought I was with Nate?" I asked softly.

There was a small chuckle. "Yeah, I was a little. I have no right to be upset or jealous, but I was. I felt stupid that you apparently had a fiancé and I didn't even know it."

"Luke, you're the only one I'm interested in. I know you don't know much about me, but I'm not like that."

"I feel like I do know a lot about you," he replied.

I smiled. "You're right. You probably know me better than anyone else at this point. I don't randomly have sex with men. I wanted what happened between us. In fact, I wouldn't mind another sleepover."

"What the hell!" my father's voice boomed so loud it nearly knocked me out of my chair. "You son of a bitch!" he roared.

I heard the chair next to me scoot back and I assumed Luke had just jumped out of his seat. I stood as well, turning towards the sound of my father's angry voice. "Sir, wait."

"You fucker! I hired you to take care of my daughter! I trusted you and you took advantage of her! I'm not paying you to sleep with her."

"Dad, it isn't like that!" I hollered, hating that I couldn't see him. Hating that I couldn't step in front of him. I knew he would be advancing on Luke, ready to hit him.

"Bullshit! You're fired! Get the fuck out of my house and don't you dare come back!"

"Mr. Sullivan," Luke started.

"Get out!"

"Dad! Relax. You're freaking out over nothing."

"No wonder Nate is upset! You've been cheating on him with the guy I hired to take care of. You have made a fool out of me and I won't tolerate it."

"I'm not cheating on Nate!" I shouted, trying to get through to my father. "Nate and I broke up the night of the accident. That's why I was driving home. Nate feels guilty. But we are through and have been for a long time. He never wanted me for me anyway. He only wanted me for your money!"

That seemed to get through and I didn't hear anything for several seconds.

"Worse," he seethed. "You come in here, preying on my little girl when she's been through something traumatic. She's in a fragile state and you took advantage of that. If you don't get out of my house in the next two seconds, I'll call the police and report you for rape."

"Rape!" Luke gasped. "What in the hell are you even talking about!"

"She didn't know what she was doing!" my dad shouted back. "My little girl was in a vulnerable state and you took advantage of it. I'm going to make you pay. You will never work in this state again. Hell, by the time I'm done with you, you'll never work anywhere again."

"Dad—"

My voice was drowned out by Luke's. "You don't even know what you're talking about. First of all, she is not a little girl. Second of all, I would never take advantage of any woman no matter what the situation was."

"Bullshit! You knew she was fresh off a breakup, coupled with the fact she's suffering from a traumatic injury. You knew and you used it to have your way with her."

"You don't know anything about your daughter," Luke hissed. "Take a minute to listen to what she wants for a change."

"I know what's best for my daughter."

"You know what's best for you. What is it that bothers you most; the fact that she's blind or the fact that she doesn't like the guy you've chosen for her?"

I winced, knowing the two of them were about to go at it. "Luke, Dad, come on, please."

"It's time you looked at her like she was an adult instead of a child to be controlled. She's smart and she can make her own decisions. She doesn't need you or Nate or me telling her what's best for her. That's her choice to make."

"Get out," my dad's voice was deadly low. It sent a chill down my spine.

"Why don't you stop trying to fix her," Luke said, his voice just as calm and menacing. "Bree isn't broken. She's pretty fucking perfect the way she is. Once you learn to accept that, maybe then she can move on with her life."

I heard footsteps and knew he had left the room. I wanted to go after him. Stepping forward, I reached out to feel my way. My dad grabbed my wrist. "Sit down, young lady. You will not chase after that man. He's not for you. He's a snake, a wolf in sheep's clothing. I'm sorry I ever brought him into your life."

"I'm not," I whispered. "I'm not one bit sorry."

"I'll find someone else. A woman. An old woman. I won't have anyone else preying on you."

"It wasn't like that. Why won't you just listen to me for once? I'm a big girl. I have been for some time now. You can't seem to understand that. I am capable of making my own decisions."

"Not in your condition. You need me."

I threw my hands up. "Dad, it's not a condition! This is it. This is me. What you see, is what you get. I'm sorry if that's not enough for you. Now, please get out of my way, I'd like to go to my room."

"You can't hide in there all the time. It isn't healthy."

I pushed around him, finding my way back to my room and slamming the door behind me. Luke was right. My father was treating me like I was broken and in need of fixing. He was the one making me feel like I was damaged goods.

Chapter Twenty-Two

Luke

I WAS SO MUCH MORE than pissed. I was fed up. I was exhausted. I felt like a human punching bag. What was it about me that made people want to use me? I wasn't feeling sorry for myself. Not at all. I truly wanted to know what I was doing that led people to believe I could be used and tossed to the side when they were finished.

Things were not going the way I had hoped. I had let myself get caught up with a woman that was not in a place in her life where she could be in a meaningful relationship. That was on me. I should have known better. Hell, I did know better, but that didn't stop me from getting caught up in it all.

I was confident Paul would follow through with his threat to ruin me. I could stay in LA and try to find work, but I had a feeling he was going to leave quite the black mark on my reputation. I could try modeling to pay the bills, but that wasn't a long-term solution.

Now I was fucked, and I had done it to myself by giving in to the desire. Now, I had to be prepared to pay the price that went along with that. I got up from the couch and walked into the kitchen. It felt strange to be at home in the middle of the day. If I were back home in Dallas, I would have things to do, errands to run that had been put off, people to see and catch up with.

But here I had nothing, and had never felt as alone as I did in that moment. At least in Texas I could have filled my time taking care of my mom. It wasn't the most pleasant thing to do, but it was something. I hated downtime. I hated not having something to do. My mother always used to tell me idle hands were the devil's tools. I knew it was part of her manipulation of me because she wanted to keep me running my ass off to serve her. I knew it and yet, it had still stuck with me.

I grabbed my phone off the counter and saw a missed call from Bree. I wasn't going to call her back. Her dad had probably already filed a police report accusing me of rape. That had been hard to hear. I had never been accused of anything so vile and I hated that he thought so little of me that he actually believed that was even possible.

There were text messages I had been ignoring as well. One was from Bree asking me to call her, and other was from Austin. I stared at Austin's message that was basically him just saying hi. Austin and I came from very different worlds, but I liked him well enough. He had asked me to hang out on more than one occasion, but I was always working.

But I wasn't working now. I wondered if he was. I didn't have rich friends. I didn't know what rich people did when they hung out. "Fuck it," I mumbled.

I needed to get out of the house or I was going to go out of my mind. I quickly texted him back and asked if he was busy for the day. He texted me back with an address and told me to head over. I figured it was better than sitting here alone.

Driving up a winding hill, the houses were growing grander with each passing driveway. I stopped, double checking the address he had given me. "Holy shit," I gasped. I turned my car into the driveway, pushing the button at the gate. I heard a quiet motor and looked up to see a camera adjusting, zooming in and out on me. Did I smile?

A second later the gate swung open. I drove forward noticing the expensive sports car parked in front of an open garage stall. I got a peek inside the garage and saw what resembled a parking garage of expensive, exotic cars. I knew he had money, but I had no idea just how wealthy he was. I debated turning around and driving right back out. I wasn't trying to date the guy, but damn, he was clearly out of my league.

I figured I should at least go in and say hi though, and I was sure it would be my only chance to ever see something so grand up close and in person. I rang the bell, listening to the majestic chimes echoing throughout the space beyond.

A man—no, a living, breathing butler—opened the door. "Good afternoon," he said in a haughty tone.

Staring at him, I nearly burst into laughter. "Hello, I'm here to see Austin."

"Yes, sir. Follow me, please."

I felt like I was a little kid in a museum. I had to remind myself not to touch anything and keep my hands to myself. I was led into a massive space that very much resembled a bar after hours. Austin was at a pool table, shooting pool by himself.

"Hey, you made it," he said, putting the cue on the table.

"I made it. This is impressive," I said, looking around the huge space. There were a few tables, a full bar with various neon beer signs hanging on the walls. It looked like an actual bar. In his house.

He chuckled. "I've found it's much easier and safer to hang out at home with a few friends than to go out to a club with strangers. Everyone has an agenda, it seems. Here I don't have to worry about being photographed doing something stupid and then blackmailed. I don't have to worry about finding a ride home or being the unwitting victim of a gold digger."

"A gilded cage," I said.

He shrugged. "I like my gilded cage. I've done my time in the trenches. I've been the subject of one scandal after another. When you're at the top, everyone wants to take you down."

I laughed. "Humble too."

"Honest."

"I suppose even the rich have problems."

"They do. But, let's talk about your problems. Want a beer?"

"I'm not at home, I have to drive."

He shrugged. "I don't know if you noticed the size of my house, but I have twenty-seven bedrooms and twice as many bathrooms, or close to it. I think I can manage to put you up for the night if need be. Come on, let's get drunk. It's been too long for me."

His offer was tempting. I needed a good drunk. "Alright. I think you're a bad influence."

He chuckled, walking behind the bar and grabbing a bottle from the shelf. I raised an eyebrow, expecting a beer. "Don't worry, it's all top shelf."

I laughed. "That was not my concern."

He poured two glasses and walked to one of the semi-circle couches that were often found in the VIP sections of clubs. I sat on one end while he sat on the other. "What's up? Why are you drinking in the middle of a work day?"

I smiled. "Because I got fired."

"Damn. That was fast. What'd you do?"

I looked around the bar, took into account everything I knew about him and decided to spill my guts. "I slept with my client."

He sputtered on the drink. "Shit. You Texas boys don't hold back."

"It wasn't like that. It isn't like that. She's special."

"Who fired you? Her? Did you do it wrong? If you need pointers, I'm your man."

I laughed. "I don't think I need pointers. It was her father that fired me. He overheard us talking and accused me of taking advantage of his daughter. I did not take advantage of her. She was a very willing partic-ipant. She came to my house."

"How old is the girl?"

"That's just it, she isn't a girl. She's a twenty-five-year-old woman, but her dad treats her like a child."

"Have you talked to her? Tried to reason with her dad?"

I shook my head. "No. It just happened."

He sipped the drink. "Do you care about her?"

"I do."

"Now that you're fired, doesn't that mean you are free to see her again?"

I scoffed. "I don't think her dad will let me within ten feet of her."

He was quiet as he sipped his drink. "Damn. I don't know man. I would say go after her, but around here, it's dangerous to cross a guy. We kind of have our own code. A man lives and breathes by his reputation around here."

"Which means I'm fucked."

"Ah, don't worry just yet. I'm sure he was pissed, but like you said, she's a big girl."

I rubbed my hand over my jaw. "Turns out she is or was engaged. Her dad likes the guy. She told me she ended things with the guy but I'm not sure what to think. He's been calling nonstop and sending flowers. In some ways, I think I got played a little."

"How did you get played?"

I thought about it. "I don't know. I feel played."

He got up and grabbed the bottle, bringing it back to the couch. "You like her. You feel like shit because she used and abused your body."

I grinned. "I guess so."

My phone rang and I thought there was a chance it could be Bree. I wanted to apologize. I couldn't be mad at her. I was the one who let my feelings get in the way.

It wasn't Bree. It was my mother. "I have to take this," I said.

"I'll give you a minute. I need to go check on some things anyway."

"Thanks." I answered the phone call. "Hello, Mom."

"Oh Luke," she whined. "Where are you?"

"Still in California, right where I've been." I was not in any mood to deal with her drama.

"I need you home, Luke. It's bad this time. Really bad."

Sitting forward, I was immediately on alert. "What's wrong?"

"I've taken a turn for the worse," she whined. "This is the worst it's ever been."

"Have you talked to your doctor?"

"Oh, you know them, they don't listen. Luke, I just want you to know I love you. If I don't make it, just know I love you and I appreciate all that you did for me."

I closed my eyes. What was I doing? She needed me. I was making a mess of my life in California. I had tried and failed miserably. "Mom, come on, it can't be all that bad."

She groaned. "It is, I promise you it is. My left arm is stiff and painful. I've been dealing with chest pain all day. I'm sure it's a heart attack or an infection that will kill me. No one will listen. You always had a way of making them listen. I understand you need to be away from me. I've kept you to myself. A mother only wants the best for her children. If you can't be happy here, I won't ask you to stay."

She was playing up the guilt. I wasn't sure she was wrong. I did leave her. I abandoned her. I cleared my throat. "Why don't I fly home for a couple days and help you get back on your feet?"

"Oh sweetie, you don't have to do that. I know you have a life for yourself. I can't ask you to sacrifice any more of your time."

I rubbed my temple. I didn't want to go home. I had left for a reason. Going back was only putting me right back in the same position I had fled. It was a risk. I knew it but her pleas for my return were getting to me. I wasn't heartless. My mother drove me crazy, but I loved her all the same.

"I'll be there soon," I said on a sigh.

Chapter Twenty-Three

Bree

I COULDN'T GET OUT of bed. Physically, I probably could, but I couldn't bring myself to do anything more than lie in bed. I had closed the blinds, not that I could see the sun, but I knew it was there. I wanted to be in the literal darkness as well as the darkness imposed on me by my blindness. My father had tried to talk to me. I couldn't deal with him.

He was hell bent on destroying any happiness I might find because he had his own agenda. He didn't know Nate. He didn't hear the things Nate had said to me. He didn't know Nate didn't love me. Nate loved the idea of me. He loved the idea of being my husband and controlling me while having access to the money and power my father wielded.

I was in a deep depression and was actually worried about myself. I had never felt so low. I had battled depression since the accident, but what I felt in that moment was so much worse. I felt physical pain. It was stupid. Luke had only been in my life a short time, but he had made it so much better. With him, I had a new kind of vision. I felt the colors. I felt the scenery. I felt the things I couldn't physically see.

And now I just missed him. More than I thought was possible. I had known him for such a short time, yet it felt like I had known him forever. I told myself it was just me being sappy, but I wasn't the sappy type. I felt things for him, but I wasn't sure it was real. Nothing felt right.

Of course, I knew there were no strings attached. Luke and I had never discussed anything about the two of us being a thing. It was just sex. We had chemistry and acted on it. He was an attractive man, according to Mel, and was new to LA. He was probably enjoying all the women and freedom. He left me every day and had his evenings and nights free. I had no idea what he did when he left the house and had never felt right asking about it.

"I'm coming in and you are not stopping me," Mel's voice flooded the darkness.

I rolled over, facing the door. "I'm in a horrible mood. Trust me, you don't want to be anywhere near me right now."

"Your dad called me."

"What?"

"You aren't taking my calls, so I knew something was wrong. Then he called me this morning."

I sighed, sitting up and brushing the hair from my face. I had yet to shower and knew my hair was probably a greasy mess. I couldn't bring myself to care. "Did he tell you why?"

"He told me he fired your murse man."

"He's not a murse," I snapped.

"What happened? Why did he fire him? Did he find out about the sleepover?"

"Actually, yes he did."

I felt her weight sink onto the bed beside me. "How did that happen?"

I quickly filled her in on the story, listening to her sounds of shock and understanding. "He hasn't called me and the few times I did call him, he sent me straight to voicemail."

"I'm sorry," she said, putting her hand on my leg.

"I'm a mess," I whispered, fresh tears flowing down my cheeks.

"You liked him?"

"It's a lot more than that. I fell for him. How dumb is that?"

"It's not dumb," she answered.

"It is dumb. I fell for him. I'm nothing more than a patient to him."

"I think you're more than that," she said.

I shook my head. "I don't think so. Look at me. I'm damaged goods. How can I expect a man to love me? He would always have to be taking care of me, making my sandwiches, picking out my clothes and leading me around stores. We couldn't go out dancing. We can't go to the beach without him holding my hand."

The despair I had felt since the accident was amplified. It had taken hold and I couldn't quite seem to find my way out of its steely grasp. "Stop it," she ordered. "Stop it right now."

"Mel, I'm not who I was!" I wailed. "I don't know what to do with myself. I sit around and sulk and cry, feeling like a lump. I don't know what to do! How can anyone love me when I don't even like myself?"

I heard her sharp intake of breath. "Enough. I'm over it. I'm done listening to you cry and moan."

"Excuse me?"

"I'm serious, Bree. You are alive. Do you know how close you came to dying? You didn't see your car, but let me tell you something, I did, and it—I can't describe how it made me feel. Your father, he collapsed when we all realized how close we had come to losing you. It nearly killed him. You know your father loves you. Yes, he's overprotective and that stubborn streak you have obviously came from him. He's going to fight like hell for you, no matter what."

"I didn't know," I whispered.

"No, you didn't know. No one wanted to talk about the accident with you, but you need to know just how bad it was so you can be grateful for being here at all. You can walk. You're not disfigured. You're not a potato trapped in a bed with a machine breathing for you. Honey, I'm sorry you lost your sight, I really am. But dammit we nearly lost you and by some miracle we didn't. Don't you dare throw that away now and die one day at a time in this room. It's time to stand up, move on and get over it!"

"Melissa! You have no idea how I feel!"

"No, I don't, but I know you're here. I know you're smart and gorgeous and funny. I know that guy has a thing for you and that when he showed up you started to smile and live a little again. You have a lot going for you but as long as you spend your energy dwelling on what you don't have, you can't enjoy it. You can't just give up. You can't just roll over and let life kick your ass."

I got up, wanting to get away from her and her words. She was being rude and hurtful. "I'm not giving up."

"You are so. You've been locked in your room for days. You can't see yourself, but damn, you look like hell. I could flip you over and wax the wood floors with the oil on your head. You are giving up. You're not even trying."

"You don't know anything about what it's like living like this," I hissed, my anger growing.

"No, I don't, but you need to pull your head out of your ass and figure out what to do next."

My jaw dropped. "Melissa! What has gotten into you? You're being awful."

"Yeah? How do you like it? I'm being awful because I love you and want my friend back. You've been in this funk and I understand why, but it's been long enough. It's time for you to come back to life. I miss you. I want to laugh with you. I want to do the things we used to."

I threw my arms up. "That's what I'm trying to tell you! I can't do the things we used to do!"

"Maybe not the same things, or the same way. But we can do new things. You've been having a good time with Luke. I can do that for you as well. I miss my friend."

I wiped my face with my hands. "Mel, I'm a mess. I don't know which way is up. It's hard to explain but every morning I wake up and

I'm lost. I don't know how to do anything. I don't know what to do with myself. I'm just so lost."

"This is going to sound terrible and I can't believe I'm saying it, but you need help. Professional help. I don't know how to help you. I don't want you to suffer but I don't know what to do to make it better. I know you're dealing with a lot. Your dad knows you are struggling. Why do you think he is trying to fix you so badly? It's all he knows how to do. Your dad, my parents, they have money. They are used to throwing money at things until it's magically all better."

She was right. I knew she was right. I had been wallowing. I hated myself for what I had become, and it wasn't just the lack of sight I hated. "I hate being a victim."

"Then stop being a victim!"

I shook my head. "You don't understand. I can't just not be a victim. I am a victim."

"You are what you choose to be."

I made a rude sound. "That's some stupid psychobabble."

"You can choose to be a victim and really get into the role or get up and decide you got the shaft and figure out how to move on."

I burst into hysterical laughter. I felt crazy. "The shaft?"

She giggled as well. "What happened sucks. It really does, but it's done. You can't go back."

I threw my head back, imagining the high ceiling in the room. "I cannot tell you how mad I am at myself for the whole thing. I am so pissed at myself for leaving just then. I keep asking myself why I stormed out at that moment. If I would have stayed another five minutes, it wouldn't have happened. If I would have just kept my mouth shut and ate the stupid Chinese and let him plan our wedding, I would be normal."

Her arms came around me. "No way. Kicking Nate to the curb was the right move. I'm not sad he's gone. We're going to get through this.

I don't know if 'we' includes Luke or not, that's up to you two, but me, you and your dad—"

I groaned. "I'm still mad at him, my Dad, I mean. He doesn't get to run my life. I'm a grown woman and can sleep with anybody I choose."

"Yes, that's true, but maybe don't tell your dad. You didn't before and I don't think it's wise to start doing it now."

I scoffed. "I didn't actually tell him about Luke, either. He was eavesdropping."

"Well, keep your sordid affairs on the down low then."

I smiled. "I'll try and remember that in the future."

"Go get showered. We're getting coffee and then we're going shopping."

"Mel, I can't go shopping. I can't see."

"I can, and I'll tell you what you're looking at. Besides, I have better taste than you do anyway. So, I get to dress you and I'm kind of looking forward to it."

"I think you're taking advantage of the situation."

"I am. I absolutely am. You'll be like my personal Barbie doll. I think I'm going to start dressing you in pink. I've always thought you would look great in pink."

I groaned. "Over my very dead body."

"There's the kicker, you'll never know what color you're wearing."

"Damn, when did you get so mean?"

"I am. Go shower now. I'm going to the kitchen to make you something to eat. You really do look like hell at the moment. When you're done eating, I'm putting some makeup on you. You look like death."

I sighed. "Because that's how I've been feeling."

"Not anymore."

I smiled. "Not anymore. Okay, I'll try harder. When I feel myself circling the drain, I'll try to pull back."

"You don't have to try alone. Reach out and let me help you. It's expected that you'll have bad days. I'm not saying you can't have bad days, but I'm saying you can't let the bad days become your new normal. You have a bad day, eat a pint of ice cream and cry your head off. Then, you get up."

Chapter Twenty-Four

Luke

I TOSSED MY SUITCASE on the bed before opening the top drawer of my dresser. I bought the ticket home with the last of my savings and hoped I wasn't making a big mistake. I felt like I was walking into the lion's den. I kept telling myself I would not get roped in to staying in Dallas. I was only packing a few things and leaving my car. That would force me to come back. At least, that's what I would tell her. I couldn't stay. I knew she would ask me to and I would tell her I had a job waiting for me. I was not above lying.

I heard my Skype ringing and leaned over to see who it was. I smirked when I saw it was Austin. I pushed the button, picking it up and waiting for his face to appear. "You're still alive!" I exclaimed.

He chuckled, tousling his hair that was a bit too long by some standards. "Barely. What time did you leave?"

"I got up early."

"Is that a Texas thing? Drink all night and be none the worse for wear in the morning?"

I laughed. "You out drank me by quite a bit lot. I did not drink nearly as much as you did."

He grinned. "Hell, that was an easy night. When I really tie one on, I don't come up for air for days."

I shook my head. "I now understand why you put a bar in your home. You clearly can't be trusted in public. Especially when you seem prone to taking off your clothes."

His deep laughter followed by a groan. "I was hot."

"I'll keep that in mind the next time we drink. I'm just glad you kept your underwear on."

He winked. "That's not always the case."

I groaned. "Good to know."

"What are you doing?" he asked, as I used my free hand to toss some stuff into the suitcase.

"I'm packing."

"Packing? Where are you going?"

I rolled my eyes. "We talked about this last night."

"And you saw me strip down to my underwear which I only vaguely remember."

"I'm going home for a couple days. My mom is sick, and I need to check on her."

"Didn't you tell me your mom was a hypochondriac?"

"What?" I asked, a little pissed that he would say something negative about my mother.

He laughed again. "Ah, so you don't hold your liquor all that well. You carried on for quite a bit about the drama back home."

"Oh," I said, a little embarrassed. "I hope I didn't bore you with all the gory details."

"Nah, I only remember bits and pieces anyway. But back to the packing, why are you going back?"

"Because she needs me."

"You're going to get sucked into a rabbit hole," he warned.

That part was right. "I'll be fine."

"It wasn't just your mother you carried on about," he said.

I groaned, vowing to never drink again. "Bree?"

He nodded. "Yep, Bree. Bree the Great. Bree, Bree, Bree."

"Sorry. I hope I didn't sound like a lovesick puppy."

"A little bit, but I think you like this girl, which makes me ask you again why it is you are running away?"

"I'm not running away, I'm visiting my mother. There's a difference."

"You should be running to Bree. If you want her, you have to fight for her."

"It has nothing to do with fighting for her," I told him. "She's not interested in a guy like me. I'm going home. When I get back, I'll start looking for a new job."

"How do you know if she's interested or not? Don't you think you should at least ask her? Maybe tell her how you feel?"

I stared at the screen, making sure it was really him I was talking to. "Why do you sound like a woman?"

He chuckled, obviously not offended by my insult. "Hey, I'm more than just a pretty face. I've been in a similar position. Unfortunately, I fucked it up. I didn't get all girly and spill my guts. Don't make the same mistake I did."

"Thanks, but I'll be fine. I need to get home."

"Are you happy?" he asked.

I looked at him like he was crazy. "What are you talking about?"

"I don't want to sound too fruity, but the few times we talked while you were working there, you seemed happy. You sure smiled a hell of a lot more."

I blew out a breath. "I *was* happy with her."

"Then why are you ditching her?"

"I'm not ditching her. Her dad isn't going to let me see her."

"Call her and have her meet you somewhere. Like you said, she's a big girl. She snuck out of the house before, she'll do it again."

I wanted to believe he was right. "Maybe when I get back."

"Have you been to the beach since you've been canned?"

I grimaced. "No. It isn't the same."

"Ha!" he shouted so loud I nearly dropped the phone. "You got it bad, I knew it! Dammit man, don't run away."

"I'm not running away," I snapped. "I have responsibilities at home. It isn't like I'm doing anything here right now."

He made a face. "You said your mom does this to you all the time. It's why you're out here to begin with. Why the hell are you running right back then? It's a trap."

"I know it's a trap, which therefore makes it not a trap. I can still visit her without having to stick around and babysit her."

"I hope so man. You're a good guy and I hate to think of you as a miserable man. Life is short. Your girl will tell you that. You have to live for you and no one else."

"I get it. I need to finish packing. My flight leaves in a couple hours."

"Fine, I'll quit nagging. I would say have fun, but we both know you're going to be miserable. Call me when you get back. I ordered a new case of whiskey, some good stuff from Scotland. We'll bust into it."

I shook my head. "How can you even think about whiskey when you look the way you do? You've got to feel like hell."

He held up a glass with some amber liquid in it. "Hair of the dog."

"Gross," I groaned. "Goodbye. I'll talk to you later."

Ending the video call, I tossed the phone on the bed. His advice, crude as it was, was good. I was supposed to be chasing my own happiness without being obligated to my mother. I knew it was risky going back and I knew my mother would only make me feel like shit for not staying, but I had to go. It wasn't like I was doing any good sitting around the way I was.

I told myself I would go, ease my mind about my mother's health and then come back and start really living again. With my mother, it was hard to know what was real and what wasn't sometimes. She put the little boy who called wolf too many times to shame. She had called wolf so many times it was expected of her.

But I would never be able to live with myself if I didn't go check on her, then found out she was truly sick. Worse, if she died without me at least getting to see her one last time in person, I would carry that guilt forever. I would never be able to find that happiness I was so desperate to have if I was forced to carry the guilt.

I tossed in a couple pairs of shorts and zipped the suitcase. I wasn't going to talk myself out of going. Carrying the suitcase out to the front door, I took care of some last-minute things before heading out. I tossed around everything Austin had said on the long drive to the airport. He was right. I was happy with Bree, and it wasn't the kind of happiness I wanted to give up.

I would take care of my mom, then I would come back and tackle the Bree situation head on. I would let her know I was interested in seeing her outside the mansion, away from her father. I wanted to spend time with her and just see where things went. It was a lot to ask but I was hoping she was willing to give us a try.

Suddenly, a case of the nerves took over. I had so little to offer her. She was the daughter of a wealthy man and likely had her own sizeable fortune. I was a jobless man with no family money. Was I being foolish to think she could actually want to be with me? Her dad obviously hated me and didn't approve. He would fight it. Hell, he might threaten to disinherit her if she pursued me.

"You're an idiot, Luke. You're a damn fool."

I sat in the airport, waiting for my flight with my phone in my hand. I wanted to text her but didn't dare. She would have to listen to it and there was always the chance her father would hear. I wasn't even sure she would want to hear from me.

Pushing it all aside, I couldn't think about all that now. It would be waiting for me when I got back. Soon my flight was called and I got in line and knew I was at a point of no return. I could still walk out of the airport and forget about going home.

"Sir?"

I blinked, saw the woman holding out her hand for my ticket and handed it over. "Thank you," I said, and walked on.

Taking my seat on the plane, I stared out the window. I hated feeling torn. I hated feeling like I had to do the right thing when all I wanted to do was the wrong thing for her and the right thing for me. It made me feel selfish. I felt like a total asshole for resenting my mother. She was my mother. She had raised me—kind of.

I truly didn't think she was capable of much more than what she had given me. She wasn't well in every sense of the word. She tried. The woman was just not meant to be a mother. It was unfortunate she'd been a mother twice over and two kids had to suffer at her hands. I didn't think we had been all that damaged, but that was only by a stroke of luck.

Settling in to the flight, I tried to close my eyes and get some rest. Once I landed in Dallas, I knew it was going to be a long couple of days. She would keep me running, doing her bidding until I collapsed from exhaustion. I was a glutton for punishment in that regard.

Chapter Twenty-Five

Bree

I WAS TRYING TO DO better. I was trying to shake off the idea that I was a victim of my circumstances, but it was ridiculously hard. I supposed once again, I only had myself to blame. I had fallen into some bad habits and it was going to be very difficult to overcome them now.

I missed my dad and the close relationship we had shared. Even before the accident I had talked to him at least once a day. He was one of my best friends. I trusted and depended on him. I hated that there was a rift between us now. I couldn't lose him. When it came right down to it, he was the only person I truly had in my life, beyond Mel. One day Mel would get married and have a family of her own. I didn't see that in my future. It was just me and my dad.

As of now, my father wasn't talking to me. Although, to be fair, I wasn't exactly talking to him, either. The iciness in the house was very uncomfortable. The only way there was going to be a thaw was if I humbled myself and sought him out.

I trailed my hand along the wall as I made my way towards his study. It was a Sunday afternoon and I expected him to be in there reading or doing whatever it was he did in there. I found the door was open, likely for my sake. He was pissed at me, but I knew if I needed him, all I had to do was call out.

"Dad?" I asked, hoping he was in the room.

I heard the sound of a newspaper dropped. "Bree? Are you okay?"

A second later his hand was on mine. "I'm fine. I was hoping we could talk."

"I'd like that," he said, taking my hand and leading me into the study. "The chair is behind you."

I smiled at the progress we had made in simple navigation. I knew he was learning how to live with me just as I was learning how to be blind. It was a huge adjustment. He struggled to remember my blindness and I struggled to remember he forgot something that dominated my every thought.

"Thank you," I said, as I slowly sat down. It was crazy how difficult it was to sit when I had no idea where the seat was. It was one of the many things I was still struggling to get used to. It was a lot of blind faith, pun intended.

"How are you, hon?" he asked.

"I'm good. You?"

"I'm well."

I licked my lips. "Dad, I'm sorry I didn't tell you about Nate. I would have told you we had broken up, but then the accident happened, and it really didn't seem all that important given everything else that was going on."

"Did he mistreat you?" he asked.

I smiled, slowly shaking my head. "No, but he wasn't the man for me. We fought all the time. I honestly think he would have preferred to marry you given the chance."

"What?" he choked out the word.

I laughed. "Not you, but your money. Nate tolerated me. He hated most everything about me. He's the kind of guy that prefers his women obedient, preferably barefoot and knocked up."

"Bree, that's a terrible thing to say."

"It's true, Dad. I thought I could change him. I thought he would eventually see that I wasn't willing to be that person. It was never going to work."

He let out a long sigh. "I didn't realize things were that bad between you."

"It's not a big deal. I want to leave Nate in my past. That's what he is to me now. He will not be part of my future."

"I have to respect that, but I have to ask, is this something that can be fixed? Is this something that needs some time maybe?"

"No. It's done."

"Okay," he said, but I could hear the reservation in his voice.

"Dad, I know you're upset about what happened at the hospital. I'm sorry for what happened. I don't want to be like this. Trust me, I'm just as embarrassed as you are. When I heard those sirens, heard the intercom and the beeping, it brought everything back from that night. I was in and out of consciousness. I don't remember a lot, but I do have snippets of memory from that night. I freaked. I'm sorry. I want to say it won't happen again, but I can't promise that."

"Oh honey, don't be sorry. I didn't realize it would trigger such painful memories. You know I would never put you in a situation that hurt you."

I nodded. "I know you wouldn't. But with that said, I am willing to try again if they'll see me."

"You know I will make that happen," he said excitedly.

"However, I need something from you before I do that."

He chuckled. "Is this a bribe? Are you trying to bargain with me?"

I grinned. "I am your daughter."

"What are your terms?" he asked, and I could hear the smile in his voice. I had missed that.

"I want you to hire Luke back," I told him, doing my best to sound firm. "And, I want you to apologize for what you said to him. And he has to go with us to the appointment."

My demands were met with silence. "I cannot allow a man into my home that did what he did to you."

"He didn't do anything to me," I replied. "What happened between us was consensual. Actually, if you want to be mad at anyone, be mad at me. I'm the one who went after him."

"Bree, I don't think it's a good idea. You may not realize it now, but you are in a very vulnerable state. You haven't been quite yourself lately and that is not your fault. It's expected. That doesn't mean you need to be taken advantage of."

"He didn't take advantage of me," I insisted. "I can't explain it, but Luke has made me feel alive again. When I'm with him, I feel like I can see. I feel like I am part of the world and not just someone lost in the shuffle. Whenever we go anywhere, he is right beside me. He tells me what's happening and makes me feel as if I'm really in the scene and not just an interloper."

"Are you saying I don't do that?

"I'm saying I don't always feel like I'm really a part of the world I'm in. I feel forgotten, ignored. I know that isn't your intention, but it's just little things that I once took for granted. When we're at breakfast and you're reading the paper like you always do, I'm struggling, Dad. I'm struggling to find my food on the plate. I can't see you. I don't even know if you're in the room anymore sometimes."

He was quiet for a bit. "I'm so sorry. I had no idea."

"And that's okay. I don't expect you to change your entire world to fit me in. I'm only saying that Luke, well, he just makes me feel normal. After you leave and we have our breakfast, we talk. I feel like he must watch me like a hawk because when he sees me reaching around, it's like he knows what I'm looking for and will give me simple cues that don't sound or feel like directions. He'll say things like 'three o'clock' or 'just an inch ahead.' It's all so inconsequential in the larger scheme, but it's so very huge to me."

He cleared his throat. "I see."

"I'm not saying you don't help me. You do. It's just different with him."

"What exactly happened between the two of you?"

I smiled. "I'm not going to give you the dirty details, but suffice it to say, I fell in love with him. I felt an immediate attraction to him from the very moment we met. Well, maybe a few moments after that, but still, there was something there."

To say it out loud was liberating. I didn't even realize it until that second. Explaining it all to my father made me realize how much I loved him. I couldn't even deal with all of that just then. I was still pleading the case with my father.

"You love him?" he questioned, with obvious shock.

"I do."

"How did this happen?"

I laughed. "I don't know. Does anyone ever know? It was a lot of little things."

"Bree, are you sure this isn't because of the situation? I don't want to say it, but you were in a vulnerable state of mind. You still are. You're not thinking clearly."

Putting up my hand, I said, "Did you hear what you said? Please don't do that. Don't discredit what I feel. If anything, it's more real than anything else I've ever experienced. I don't have the benefit of sight, which means I had to fall in love with the man for who he was. I don't know what he looks like and I don't care. It's completely different."

"Oh Bree, I want the best for you, but this guy, I don't know. You know nothing about him."

"I know a lot about him. What do you think we do all day?"

He made a choking sound. "I honestly have no idea, and I'm not certain I want to find out."

"Dad! Not that. We talk. We spend hours and hours talking. When we aren't talking, we're just kind of being. I don't expect you to understand how I feel, but I am asking you to respect it. I'm not a little girl with a crush. This is the real thing."

"If this is the real thing, where is he? Why hasn't he come around?"

"Um, maybe because you accused him of being a rapist, which by the way was very wrong. That was uncalled for and by the way, also completely inaccurate."

"I'm not sure about this," he said.

"Dad, it doesn't matter. It's my life. You want me to see the doctors and I will, if you agree to my terms."

"I can't believe you are negotiating with me. Blackmailing me, actually. I'm afraid I've created a monster."

I smiled. "Well?"

He groaned. "Fine, I'll call him tomorrow."

"Thank you. I want you to like him. He really is a good guy."

"I will hire him, but that doesn't mean I have to like him. You are still my little girl and as far as I'm concerned, he violated my trust by doing what he did."

"It was me, Dad. Blame me. I basically snuck out and went to his house. I got his information from you, remember?"

"How did you get it from me?"

I wrinkled my nose. "I might have enlisted the help of someone else's eyes, but that doesn't matter. I wanted to see him outside of this house. I can assure you he was very professional while he was here and on duty. Nothing ever happened."

"Well, I suppose you are old enough to make your own decisions in that regard, but I am not going to say I like it. I will talk with him and explain my expectations. He is supposed to be a caregiver and while he is in this house acting as such, I will hold him to certain standards."

I nodded, knowing I had pushed it far enough. "Thank you. That's all I ask."

"I'm going to call the doctors. What do I need to do to prepare you for the next appointment? Should I ask if they can come here?"

"No, I'll be okay. If Luke is there, I'll be okay."

"I feel quite inadequate when you say that."

"You are not inadequate by any means. Maybe it's his training and experience, but he has a way of calming me. He'll help me block out the terror I feel when I walk into that hospital. I'm confident I can do it if he is with me. And you too, Dad. I need you as well."

"Alright. You always knew just what to say to wrap me around your little finger."

I smiled and slowly stood. "I am not your spoiled princess for nothing. Now, while we're at it, can we talk about me getting a new car?"

"What?" he sputtered, clearly flummoxed.

"Gotcha!"

He laughed softly before leading me out of the study. "Let's get some lunch."

I was happy to have made peace with him. I knew I would sleep better. Now, it was time to reach out to Luke. I had avoided trying to before because I didn't think there was much of a point. But if my father was willing to give him his job back and apologize, I was sure he would come back.

Honestly, I needed him to come back. I needed him to see me through what was sure to be a very scary time. He just made me feel stronger in every way. He empowered me somehow and made me feel like I could do anything. I was going to tell him how I felt and hoped like hell he felt the same way.

Chapter Twenty-Six

Luke

NERVOUS AS HELL WAS the only way to describe how I was feeling. I had long debated how best to handle the situation with Bree, and decided the best thing to do was face Paul man-to-man and apologize. I wanted and needed his respect and approval. Bree and her father were too close for me to interfere with that relationship. She needed him and had made it very clear how much he needed her. I wouldn't be the one to come between that.

I wasn't sure if I would be welcomed at the mansion. Hell, I knew I wouldn't be welcomed, but I was hoping for five minutes of his time. If he refused to talk to me, I would have to defy him and reach out to Bree. I needed her to know how I felt. I needed her to know I wasn't just a guy that slept with women and then never spoke to them again. I wasn't like that.

Pulling my car into the driveway of the mansion, I had come to think of as a second home. It was a little strange to be back after being in Dallas and in my old life for a few days. I was glad I had come back to California. It had been difficult to leave my mother a second time, but knowing Bree was here was the incentive I needed. I had two women that needed me, on opposite sides of the country. But only one truly needed me, and I only wanted to be with her.

I parked my car, half-expecting there to be a bouncer ready to toss me to the curb. I slowly walked towards the front door, pausing about ten feet from the door to rehearse what I planned to say. I knew I was going to have to talk fast and wanted to make sure I said the right things. I couldn't afford to mess this up.

My phone vibrated in my pocket, giving me a perfect excuse to stall. I pulled it out and stared at the screen before looking up at the mansion and back at my screen. I knew there were security cameras all over. Had Paul seen me? Was he calling to tell me to get back in my car and leave? It was go time. It was now or never. I had to man up, apologize and hope he would give me a chance if I wanted a meaningful relationship with Bree. Fuck if I knew if she even wanted it. I could be throwing myself on the sword for nothing.

"Hello," I answered, my voice deep and manly—I hoped.

"Luke, this is Paul Sullivan," he said, as if I wouldn't know who he was.

"Yes, sir."

"I was wondering if you could come by the house so we could talk," he said.

Looked at the front door, then my car, I figured it was stupid to turn away now. "Sir, uh, I'm outside right now."

"Outside where?"

"Your front door."

"Oh." There was a pause. "I'll be right there."

Slipping the phone back into my pocket, I gave myself a pep talk. I wasn't used to talking to angry fathers. I had been a good kid. I had been a good man, never breaking the rules or coloring outside the lines. This was uncharted territory for me.

The door opened and Paul stepped out. "My study, please."

"Is Bree here?" I asked.

"She is, but I would appreciate it if you and I could have a chat before you talk to her."

I nodded, taking the win for what it was. He wasn't forbidding me from talking to her which was a good sign. "Thank you."

Following him through the house, my eyes drifted toward her closed door. I wondered if she was in her room or in the dining room like she would normally be. I longed to see her. I had missed her something fierce and could barely hold myself back from going to her.

"Have a seat," he said, gesturing to one of the leather tub chairs.

I sat down while he closed the door. That wasn't a good sign, but I was prepared to fight for her. I didn't want to alienate him, but if it came to that, I would.

"Paul, I want to apologize for being unprofessional, but I need you to understand that I would never take advantage of your daughter, or of anyone else for that matter. I'm not that kind of a man. I know you don't truly know me, but I promise you, I have never, nor would I ever push myself onto a vulnerable woman."

"I know."

I blinked, ready to continue my defense and confused at the apparent change of circumstance. I'd been all prepared with references and reasons, prepared to fight.

"Wait. You know?"

"I had a long talk with Bree, and she explained the situation a little better for me. I'm sorry for accusing you of behavior that is not in your character. I have to confess, I'm very protective of her. Overly so, perhaps. She is still my little girl and I don't want her hurt."

"I would never hurt her," I insisted. "Not intentionally. I care about her a great deal and I want to be in her life."

He slowly nodded. "I believe you. The Bree you know is not the Bree I know. She's different. My daughter was a fiercely independent woman who lived freely. She lived her life to the fullest. She was always happy and smiling and going from one adventure to another. Seeing her as she is now is difficult. I see her as fragile and as you said, broken, and I'm trying to fix her. Only because I think there is a chance. I know my daughter and I know that deep down she is a fighter. If there is any chance she can have her old life back, I want her to have it. She can do with it as she will, but I need to know if there is a chance."

"I understand that, sir. But if there isn't a chance, she needs your acceptance. She's struggling to feel like a normal person as it is. She doesn't want to disappoint you or have you think of her as somehow incomplete."

He smiled. "I know. I get it. I've not been great at dealing with the situation. She told me."

I grinned, imagining my Bree standing up for herself. "That's a start."

"It is."

"I understand that my job is gone, but I would like to see her. It just so happens I am between jobs at the moment and would very much like to spend some time with her."

He blew out a breath. "As it turns out, my daughter has demanded that I hire you back."

"She did?" I asked with surprise.

"I told you, when she wants something, she fights for it. Apparently, she wants you in her life. I will let her fill you in on all the reasons why, but she hasn't been the same since you've been gone. I hate to see her suffer and she is most certainly suffering."

I winced. "Sir, I don't think I can take your money for spending time with the woman I care about."

"I suggest you figure out how to make peace with it, because it was among the terms of our agreement," he said, in a very business-like tone.

"Our agreement?" I questioned, wondering if he was referring to my initial contract.

"No, I meant the agreement I made with my daughter which she negotiated quite ruthlessly. In exchange for me apologizing to you and hiring you back while looking the other way while the two of you do whatever it is you do, she will go to the specialist."

"Really?"

"Really. However, among the terms, she has also insisted that you go along for the visit. She doesn't believe she can face the situation without you by her side. Apparently, you give her strength. For that, I am grateful. I was happy with the change I saw in her when you were around. I caught glimpses of my daughter, the one I lost on that night, and I would like to see more of her. If that means you stick around, so be it."

He wasn't exactly thrilled with the situation; that much was clear. But I didn't care. I didn't want to kiss him and take him to bed. I just needed his blessing so I could have his daughter. "Sir, I care about her. I care about her a lot, and I really don't want your money. You can tell her you're paying me if you need to, but I will be there for her no matter what. I want to be with her."

He smiled. "I appreciate that. I really do. Take good care of her. She's my little girl, no matter how old she gets. I've made the appointment for this week. Are you able to make it?"

"Absolutely!"

He chuckled. "Good to know. Now, I'm sure you're anxious to see Bree. When she finds out you're here and I've been monopolizing your time, she's probably going to yell at me again."

I grinned. "Thank you." I hopped up from the chair. Now that I had his blessing, nothing would stop me from getting to her. I left the study and took long strides towards her bedroom. I knocked once and waited.

"Not until you call him," Bree called out.

I smiled. She was holding strong to her deal with her father. I was happy as hell she was fighting for me. I was going to fight like hell for her as well. I opened the door and walked inside. She was facing the window as usual. Her long hair was left loose and hanging over the back of the chair. One of her audiobooks was playing as she absorbed the sunlight. She was my little sun goddess. I couldn't wait to take her to the beach. I could kiss her and do all the things I had been longing to do with her.

"Did you call him?" she asked, without turning around.

"He did," I answered.

She jumped out of her chair and spun around. "Luke?"

I crossed the room and wrapped my arms around her, lifting her up as I hugged her against me. Her hands went to my face, her way of verifying it was me. "Hi," I whispered.

Her mouth slammed over mine. I kissed her with all the pent-up passion I had been holding back for a week. I never wanted to let her go. When we had finally taken the edge off, I slid her body down mine, letting her feet touch the floor. "You're back," she breathed.

I touched her face, staring into the clear blue eyes that were so gorgeous. "I'm back."

"Did you talk to my dad?"

"He did," Paul said from the door.

I turned to face him, Bree still in my arms. "We talked," I confirmed.

"It's settled? You're back? You'll be my caregiver again?"

I winced. "I'm not sure if caregiver is the term I'm going with, but I will be here with you."

"Okay," she breathed the word like she had been holding her breath for too long.

"I'll leave you two alone. I'm trusting her to your care."

"I'll take care of her," I promised.

"Thank you, Dad," Bree called out.

"Anything for you sweetheart, anything. If you're happy, I'm happy. All I want is for you to be happy. Oh and if you're wondering how he got here so fast, he was already on the front porch when I called him."

He left the room, closing the door behind him. I wasn't going to lie and say it wasn't a little awkward, but any weirdness I felt was easily ignored with her in my arms. "I've missed you," I told her.

"You have no idea how much I have missed you. What they say about not knowing what you've got until it's gone is true."

I chuckled. "I agree. How have you been?"

She sighed. "Not great, but I'm better now."

"Bree, I care so much about you. I want you to know I told your father I don't want to be paid. I don't want to be the hired help. I want to be here to be with you."

There was a soft smile on her lips. "I want you with me. I want to be with you."

"Can we say this is the start of something real?" I asked hopefully.

"Yes. I don't know if it's technically the start because I've felt this way for a while."

I kissed her again. "Me too. Have you had breakfast?"

She smiled. "No, I haven't. I've been waiting for you."

"I'm here now and it isn't going to be easy to get rid of me."

She laughed. "Good."

Chapter Twenty-Seven

Bree

LUKE'S HAND HELD MINE as we sat in uncomfortable chairs in the waiting room of the new specialist. It had been difficult, but manageable to get to the fourth floor of the building. The sirens were there and all the other triggers, but Luke helped me through it. He talked to me the entire time, helping me block out the noises that brought back terrifying memories.

The quiet chatter of conversations around us was surprisingly soothing. I focused on Luke's breathing, keeping myself calm. I didn't want to see the doctor. I had a bad feeling and couldn't quite shake it. I was only there because I had made the deal with my dad. I would have found a way to back out of it if there hadn't been a deal in place.

"Dr. Watson is one of the top neuro specialists in the world," my father said in a low voice. "I'm reading a magazine article about him. He's done some great things."

"How convenient. A magazine touting him as one of the best doctors in the world happens to be right here in his office," I replied.

Luke squeezed my hand. "I did my research on him as well. He's good."

"Let's hope he's walk-on-water good because the other doctors have all said nothing short of a miracle would bring my sight back."

"Miracles happen," Luke said. "You don't know until you do."

"Miss Sullivan?" I heard my name called and almost threw up on the spot.

This was the moment I had been looking forward to and dreading at the same time. I knew this doctor was my last shot at being able to see again. If he told me no, that was it. I had told myself I was ready for a bad outcome, but dammit if I couldn't keep myself from hoping he would say I was a perfect candidate and would see again.

"Let's go," Luke said, tugging me up.

My grip on his hand was so tight I almost lost feeling in my fingers. He didn't seem to mind as he escorted me into what I presumed was the doctor's office.

"Hello," I heard an unfamiliar male voice. "I'm Doctor Watson."

"Nice to meet you, Dr. Watson. I'm Paul Sullivan, this is my daughter Bree and her," there was a pause.

"My boyfriend, Luke Turner," I finished.

"It's nice to meet you all. Please have a seat."

Luke helped me into another chair that felt just like the kind that had been in the waiting room. I released Luke's hand, stretching my fingers and trying to regain the blood flow I had cut off. My palms were sweating as were my armpits. Thank goodness someone had invented deodorant. I hoped I didn't have sweat on my forehead.

"Thank you for taking the time to meet with us," my father said.

"Of course. Now, I've reviewed the chart and studied the various tests and talked with the doctors that initially treated you."

I slowly nodded, reaching out for Luke's hand again. I could hear the regret in the man's voice. Another benefit to being sightless, was that I heard the little nuances in a person's voice and speech like I had never been able to before. So, I already knew what was coming, and braced myself.

"And?" my father prompted.

"And I'm sorry, but I have to concur with the initial doctor's findings," he said. "The risk is too great. I know that's not what you wanted to hear, and I am truly sorry that I have to give you this news."

The air rushed from my lungs. I had been expecting it, but actually hearing the words felt like a knife to my heart. Luke squeezed my hand before scooting his chair closer to mine, his shoulder rubbing against my own. I could hear my father's breathing change as well. Actually, I could have heard a pin drop in that moment.

"What?" my father snapped. "What do you mean? You're supposed to be the best. I talked with you several times and you were very hopeful."

The doctor cleared his throat. "I can do a lot of things, sir. And I have operated on people who were told no, but in this case, I feel it is far too risky. The chance of being able to restore sight is there, though extremely slim, but the risk—the risk of doing real damage—it's very high. Too high. I can't put myself in that position and I would never put a patient in that kind of situation. When I spoke with you, I didn't have all the information."

My father sputtered. "But I sent over everything!"

"Dad," I said, hearing his temper rising.

"This is cruel. You got my hopes up. You got her hopes up. You've wasted my time."

The doctor cleared his throat. "Mr. Sullivan, I understand you're angry, but it was a Hail Mary from the very beginning. I did tell you that. I was hoping I could help, but it's just too complicated to be safe."

"There's nothing you can do?" Luke pressed.

"I'm afraid not."

I heard my father release a loud sigh. He was crushed, just as I knew he would be. The urge to run from the room was strong. I wanted to go home. I wanted to return to the safety and comfort of my bedroom. I wanted to forget I ever agreed to see the damn doctor.

"I see," my father said, and the disappointment in his voice tore at my heart. "I'm sorry to have wasted everyone's time."

"It's okay, Dad. We knew it wasn't likely. Like he said, it was a Hail Mary and it didn't work out for us."

"I'm so sorry, Bree," he choked out the words. "I'm sorry."

"I too am sorry to deliver the bad news. There is hope that there will be options in the future. Technology is always advancing, and I will definitely keep your chart in mind. In fact, I'm attending a conference next month. Maybe I'll learn something new. I'm not giving up completely.

I scoffed. "Sure. Thanks anyway, but I'm done with the hoping."

Getting up, I pulled Luke up with me. I wanted out. I wanted to run. I couldn't be in this room another second. My father's disappointment was killing me. I knew he didn't realize it, but I could feel his emotion. I could feel how devastated he was. I couldn't deal with his feelings on top of my own.

Luke led me out of the room. "You okay?" he asked softly.

I faced him, knowing he was probably studying my face. "No," I whispered. "I'm not okay. Let's go home. Please."

He gave me a hug. "We'll do that. For what it's worth, I'm sorry I encouraged you to come."

"I'm so sorry Bree," my father said from behind me. "I wanted this so badly for you. You tried to tell me. I never wanted to cause you more pain. I'm sorry."

Swallowing the lump of emotion in my throat, I knew I had to be strong for him. I could hear him falling apart. He had hoped so desperately. He had hoped with everything he had, and I knew what it felt like to be let down. He was going to crumble.

"Dad, I'm okay. We knew this was a strong possibility. I'm good. I'm ready to talk with that woman from the blind association and start moving forward."

I heard a choked sob. "I'll call her," he said. "If you'll excuse me for a minute, I'll catch up with you guys downstairs."

Waiting a few seconds, I turned back towards Luke who had a strong arm around me. "He's crushed, isn't he?"

"He'll be okay," Luke assured me. "I think he had convinced himself this was going to work. I'll be here for you. We'll get through this."

I nodded, a tear slipping from the corner of my eye. "I know."

"Excuse me," I heard a woman say.

I turned in the direction of the voice.

"Yes?" Luke said, before sucking in a breath.

"Ellis?" I heard him say with a great deal of excitement. "Ellis Tanner?"

I heard the woman's soft laughter and wanted to slap her. It was a flirty laugh. I didn't know who she was, but it was clear she was flirting with Luke.

"That's me, Dr. Tanner now, actually."

"Wow. I haven't seen you in forever."

"Not since that party," she laughed again.

I was going to accidently knock this woman out. Luke's arm was still around me, yet the woman was openly flirting. She was out of her damn mind if she thought I was going to let a little blindness keep me from fighting for my man.

"Are you working here?" he asked.

"I am. Actually, I wanted to talk with you, Gabrielle. You're Gabrielle Sullivan, right?"

"Who are you?" my father said from my other side.

"My name's Dr. Tanner. I was hoping we could chat for a minute."

"About?" my dad asked.

"Why don't we step into my office? I'm just down the hall."

"It's all good," Luke said.

I was going to let him know exactly how I felt about that once we were alone. I felt him pulling me along and knew we were going into the office. I wasn't in the mood to listen to them play catch up.

"Have a seat," the woman said.

Once again, I was shuffled into a seat. I knew I had a stormy look on my face and didn't care. I was feeling rather bitchy at the moment.

"What's going on, Ellis?" Luke asked.

"Yes, please, what's this about? We were on our way out."

"I know Dr. Watson and he's an excellent doctor, but he tends to be safe. He doesn't like taking chances."

"Considering he's talking about my daughter's life, I appreciate him being unwilling to risk it."

"You're right there, but he discussed your case with me, asking my opinion. I've seen your tests and looked at every detail and I have to say, I don't completely agree with him."

"What does that mean?" Luke asked hopefully.

"It means, I'd like to do another MRI."

"Why?" I asked. "I've already had two recently and who knows how many before that."

"But that was over a month ago. I'm going to be looking for any changes. I believe there is a different technique I can use that could give you your sight back."

I shook my head. "No way. I'm tired of hearing what doctors think they can do only to find out they can't. We've been through enough. I'm not a guinea pig."

"Bree, wait," my father said.

"Dad, I agreed to meet with your specialist. I did that. I don't know this woman and neither do you."

"I do," Luke said.

"Really? How? From a party? Is that supposed to be some kind of glowing medical reference? It's my head she wants to get into."

"We were in med school together," he answered, taking my hand back in his. "She was always the brainiac at the top of the class."

I licked my lips, still not convinced. "Why do you think you're special? What makes you think you can do something no other doctor has been able to? If you went to school with Luke, that means you have almost no experience, right? You're fresh out of school and you want me to let you into my brain?"

"Bree," my father hissed. "I'd like to hear what she has to say."

"Then you sit and listen. I fulfilled our agreement. I don't want to keep going down this road and getting kicked in the gut."

"Bree, I know it's difficult, but will you please listen to what she is proposing? For me if not for yourself?" Luke said, his face inches from my ear.

Everything was telling me not to do it. Not to set myself up for another major disappointment. The two most important people in my life were asking me to stay. How could I ignore that?

Yet how could I put myself through another gut-wrenching disappointment?

THE END

Blind Sight Series

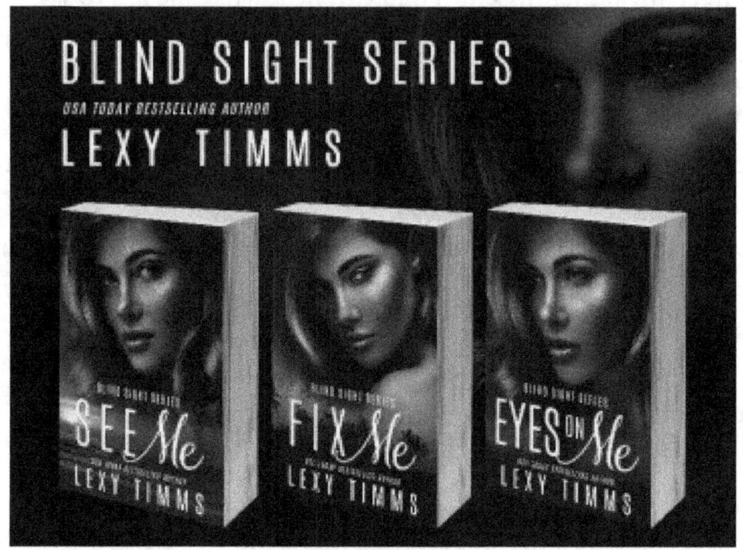

Book 1 – See Me
Book 2 – Fix Me
Book 3 – Eyes on Me

Find Lexy Timms:

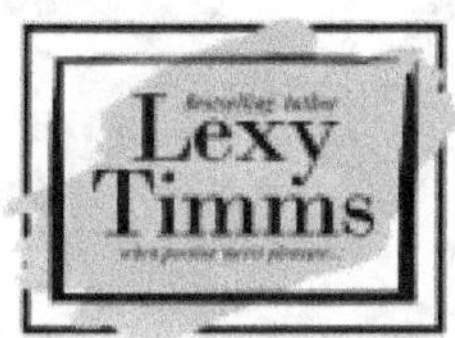

LEXY TIMMS NEWSLETTER:
http://eepurl.com/9i0vD
Lexy Timms Facebook Page:
https://www.facebook.com/SavingForever
Lexy Timms Website:
http://www.lexytimms.com

Lexy Timms
Managing BOSSES
Books 1-3
BOSS Book 3
BOSS Book 2
BOSS Book 1
FREE
for a
Limited
Time

Want

# FREE READS?

Sign up for Lexy Timms' newsletter
And she'll send you updates on new releases,
ARC copies of books and a whole lotta fun!
Sign up for news and updates!
http://eepurl.com/9i0vD

More by Lexy Timms:

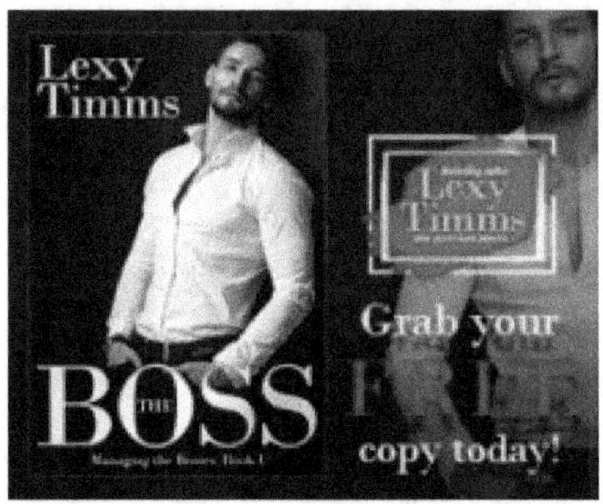

FROM BEST SELLING AUTHOR, Lexy Timms, comes a billionaire romance that'll make you swoon and fall in love all over again.

Jamie Connors has given up on men. Despite being smart, pretty, and just slightly overweight, she's a magnet for the kind of guys that don't stay around.

Her sister's wedding is at the foreground of the family's attention. Jamie would be fine with it if her sister wasn't pressuring her to lose weight so she'll fit in the maid of honor dress, her mother would get off her case and her ex-boyfriend wasn't about to become her brother-in-law.

Determined to step out on her own, she accepts a PA position from billionaire Alex Reid. The job includes an apartment on his property and gets her out of living in her parent's basement.

Jamie must balance her life and somehow figure out how to manage her billionaire boss, without falling in love with him.

** The Boss is book 1 in the Managing the Bosses series. All your questions won't be answered in the first book. It may end on a cliff hanger.

For mature audiences only. There are adult situations, but this is a love story, NOT erotica.

Faking It Description:

HE GROANED. THIS WAS torture. Being trapped in a room with a beautiful woman was just about every man's fantasy, but he had to remember that this was just pretend.

Allyson Smith has crushed on her boss for years, but never dared to make a move. When she finds herself without a date to her brother's upcoming wedding, Allyson tells her family one innocent white lie: that she's been dating her boss. Unfortunately, her boss discovers her lie, and insists on posing as her boyfriend to escort her to the wedding.

Playboy billionaire Dane Prescott always has a new heiress on his arm, but he can't get his assistant Allyson out of his head. He's fought his attraction to her, until he gets caught up in her scheme of a fake relationship.

One passionate weekend with the boss has Allyson Smith questioning everything she believes in. Falling for a wealthy playboy like Dane is against the rules, but if she's just faking it what's the harm?

A chance meeting with one of the company photographers may turn into more than just an impromptu photo shoot.

Book One is FREE!

SOMETIMES THE HEART needs a different kind of saving... find out if Charity Thompson will find a way of saving forever in this hospital setting Best-Selling Romance by Lexy Timms

Charity Thompson wants to save the world, one hospital at a time. Instead of finishing med school to become a doctor, she chooses a different path and raises money for hospitals – new wings, equipment, whatever they need. Except there is one hospital she would be happy to never set foot in again—her fathers. So of course, he hires her to create a gala for his sixty-fifth birthday. Charity can't say no. Now she is working in the one place she doesn't want to be. Except she's attracted to Dr. Elijah Bennet, the handsome playboy chief.

Will she ever prove to her father that's she's more than a med school dropout? Or will her attraction to Elijah keep her from repairing the one thing she desperately wants to fix?

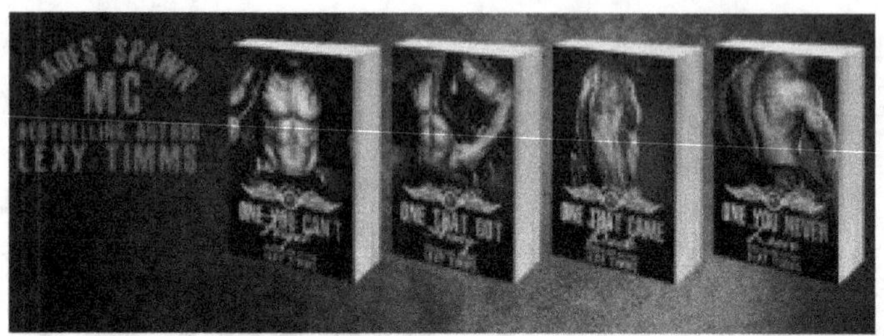

THE ONE YOU CAN'T FORGET

Emily Rose Dougherty is a good Catholic girl from mythical Walkerville, CT. She had somehow managed to get herself into a heap trouble with the law, all because an ex-boyfriend has decided to make things difficult.

Luke "Spade" Wade owns a Motorcycle repair shop and is the Road Captain for Hades' Spawn MC. He's shocked when he reads in the paper that his old high school flame has been arrested. She's always been the one he couldn't forget.

Will destiny let them find each other again? Or what happens in the past, best left for the history books?

** *This is book 1 of the Hades' Spawn MC Series. All your questions may not be answered in the first book.*

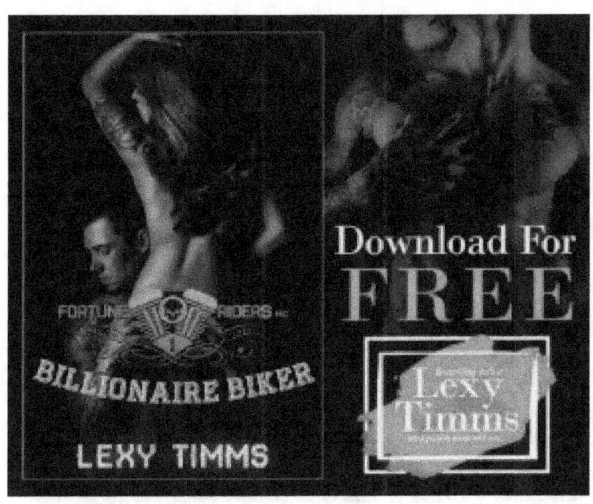

Download For
FREE
Lexy Timms

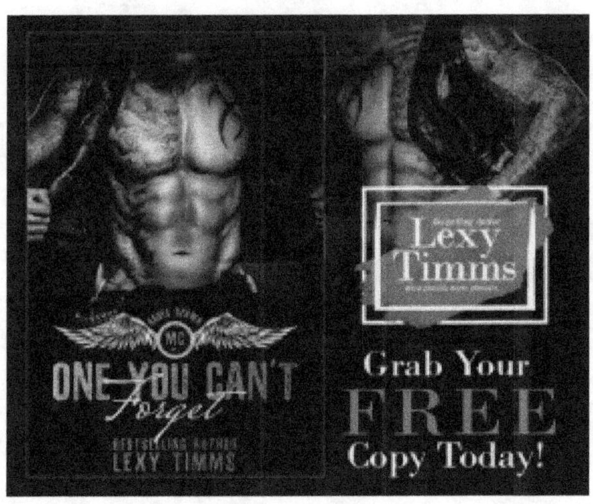

Lexy Timms
Grab Your
FREE
Copy Today!

A Burning Love Series

Book 1 – Spark of Passion
Book 2 – Flame of Desire
Book 3 – Blaze of Ecstasy

A Maybe Series

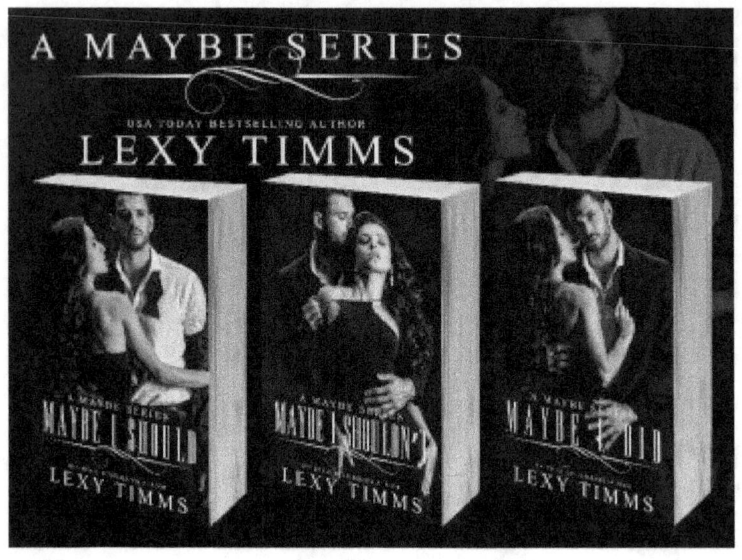

Book 1 – Maybe I Should
Book 2 – Maybe I Shouldn't
Book 3 – Maybe I Did

Darkest Night Series

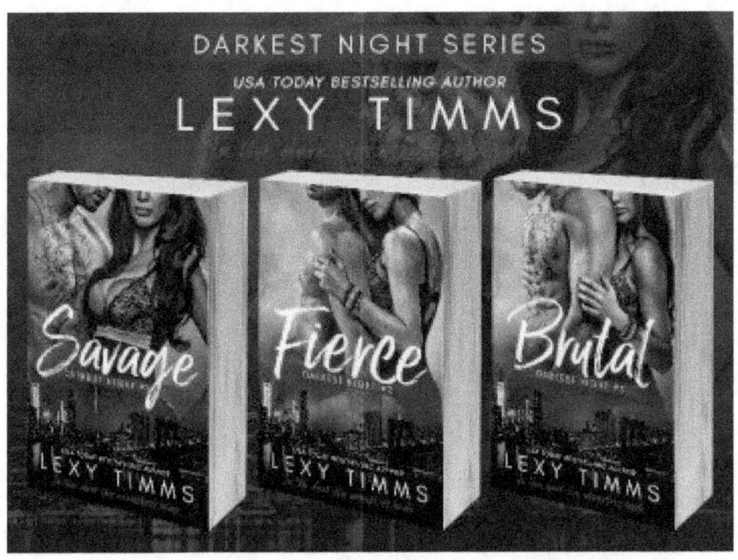

Book 1 – Savage
Book 2 – Fierce
Book 3 – Brutal

Don't miss out!

Visit the website below and you can sign up to receive emails whenever Lexy Timms publishes a new book. There's no charge and no obligation.

https://books2read.com/r/B-A-NNL-VXZDB

BOOKS 2 READ

Connecting independent readers to independent writers.

Also by Lexy Timms

A Bad Boy Bullied Romance
I Hate You
I Hate You A Little Bit
I Hate You A Little Bit More

A Burning Love Series
Spark of Passion
Flame of Desire
Blaze of Ecstasy

A Chance at Forever Series
Forever Perfect
Forever Desired
Forever Together

A Dating App Series
I've Been Matched
You've Been Matched

We've Been Matched

A "Kind of" Billionaire
Taking a Risk
Safety in Numbers
Pretend You're Mine

A Maybe Series
Maybe I Should
Maybe I Shouldn't
Maybe I Did

BBW Romance Series
Capturing Her Beauty
Pursuing Her Dreams
Tracing Her Curves

Beating the Biker Series
Making Her His
Making the Break
Making of Them

Billionaire Banker Series
Banking on Him

Price of Passion
Investing in Love
Knowing Your Worth
Treasured Forever
Banking on Christmas

Billionaire Holiday Romance Series
Driving Home for Christmas
The Valentine Getaway
Cruising Love

Billionaire in Disguise Series
Facade
Illusion
Charade

Billionaire Secrets Series
The Secret
Freedom
Courage
Trust
Impulse
Billionaire Secrets Box Set Books #1-3

Blind Sight Series
See Me

Diamond in the Rough Anthology
Billionaire Rock
Billionaire Rock - part 2

Dirty Little Taboo Series
Flirting Touch
Denying Pleasure
Forbidding Desire
Craving Passion

Dominating PA Series
Her Personal Assistant - Part 1
Her Personal Assistant Box Set

Fake Billionaire Series
Faking It
Temporary CEO
Caught in the Act
Never Tell A Lie
Fake Christmas
Fake Billionaire Box Set #1-3

Firehouse Romance Series
Caught in Flames

Burning With Desire
Craving the Heat
Firehouse Romance Complete Collection

Forging Billions Series
Dirty Money
Petty Cash
Payment Required

For His Pleasure
Elizabeth
Georgia
Madison

Fortune Riders MC Series
Billionaire Biker
Billionaire Ransom
Billionaire Misery

Fragile Series
Fragile Touch
Fragile Kiss
Fragile Love

Great Temptation Series
The Devil's Footsteps
Heaven's Command
Mortals Surrender

Hades' Spawn Motorcycle Club
One You Can't Forget
One That Got Away
One That Came Back
One You Never Leave
One Christmas Night
Hades' Spawn MC Complete Series

Hard Rocked Series
Rhyme
Harmony
Lyrics

Heart of Stone Series
The Protector
The Guardian
The Warrior

Heart of the Battle Series

Celtic Viking
Celtic Rune
Celtic Mann
Heart of the Battle Series Box Set

Heistdom Series
Master Thief
Goldmine
Diamond Heist
Smile For Me
Your Move
Green With Envy
Saving Money

Highlander Wolf Series
Pack Run
Pack Land
Pack Rules

How To Love A Spy
The Secret
The Secret Life
The Secret Wife

Just About Series
About Love

Managing the Billionaire
Never Enough
Worth the Cost
Secret Admirers
Chasing Affection
Pressing Romance
Timeless Memories

Managing the Bosses Series
The Boss
The Boss Too
Who's the Boss Now
Love the Boss
I Do the Boss
Wife to the Boss
Employed by the Boss
Brother to the Boss
Senior Advisor to the Boss
Forever the Boss
Christmas With the Boss
Billionaire in Control
Billionaire Makes Millions
Billionaire at Work
Precious Little Thing
Priceless Love
Valentine Love
Gift for the Boss - Novella 3.5
Managing the Bosses Box Set #1-3

Model Mayhem Series
Shameless
Modesty
Imperfection

Moment in Time
Highlander's Bride
Victorian Bride
Modern Day Bride
A Royal Bride
Forever the Bride

My Best Friend's Sister
Hometown Calling
A Perfect Moment
Thrown in Together

My Darker Side Series
Darkest Hour
Time to Stop
Against the Light

Neverending Dream Series
Neverending Dream - Part 1

Neverending Dream - Part 2
Neverending Dream - Part 3
Neverending Dream - Part 4
Neverending Dream - Part 5

Outside the Octagon
Submit
Fight
Knockout

Protecting Diana Series
Her Bodyguard
Her Defender
Her Champion
Her Protector
Her Forever

Protecting Layla Series
His Mission
His Objective
His Devotion

Racing Hearts Series
Rush
Pace
Fast

Regency Romance Series
The Duchess Scandal - Part 1
The Duchess Scandal - Part 2

Reverse Harem Series
Primals
Archaic
Unitary

RIP Series
Track the Ripper
Hunt the Ripper
Pursue the Ripper

R&S Rich and Single Series
Alex Reid
Parker

Saving Forever
Saving Forever - Part 1
Saving Forever - Part 2
Saving Forever - Part 3
Saving Forever - Part 4
Saving Forever - Part 5

Saving Forever - Part 6
Saving Forever Part 7
Saving Forever - Part 8
Saving Forever Boxset Books #1-3

Shifting Desires Series
Jungle Heat
Jungle Fever
Jungle Blaze

Sin Series
Payment for Sin
Atonement Within
Declaration of Love

Southern Romance Series
Little Love Affair
Siege of the Heart
Freedom Forever
Soldier's Fortune

Spanked Series
Passion
Playmate
Pleasure

Spelling Love Series
The Author
The Book Boyfriend
The Words of Love

Taboo Wedding Series
He Loves Me Not
With This Ring
Happily Ever After

Tattooist Series
Confession of a Tattooist
Surrender of a Tattooist
Heart of a Tattooist
Hopes & Dreams of a Tattooist

Tennessee Romance
Whisky Lullaby
Whisky Melody
Whisky Harmony

The Bad Boy Alpha Club
Battle Lines - Part 1
Battle Lines

The Brush Of Love Series
Every Night
Every Day
Every Time
Every Way
Every Touch

The Debt
The Debt: Part 1 - Damn Horse
The Debt: Complete Collection

The Fire Inside Series
Dare Me
Defy Me
Burn Me

The Golden Mail
Hot Off the Press
Extra! Extra!
Read All About It
Stop the Press
Breaking News
This Just In

The Lucky Billionaire Series
Lucky Break
Streak of Luck
Lucky in Love

The Sound of Breaking Hearts Series
Disruption
Destroy
Devoted

The University of Gatica Series
The Recruiting Trip
Faster
Higher
Stronger
Dominate
No Rush
University of Gatica - The Complete Series

T.N.T. Series
Troubled Nate Thomas - Part 1
Troubled Nate Thomas - Part 2
Troubled Nate Thomas - Part 3

Undercover Series
Perfect For Me
Perfect For You
Perfect For Us

Unknown Identity Series
Unknown
Unpublished
Unexposed
Unsure
Unwritten
Unknown Identity Box Set: Books #1-3

Unlucky Series
Unlucky in Love
UnWanted
UnLoved Forever

War Torn Letters Series
My Sweetheart
My Darling
My Beloved

Wet & Wild Series

Stormy Love
Savage Love
Secure Love

Worth It Series
Worth Billions
Worth Every Cent
Worth More Than Money

You & Me - A Bad Boy Romance
Just Me
Touch Me
Kiss Me

Standalone
Wash
Loving Charity
Summer Lovin'
Love & College
Billionaire Heart
First Love
Frisky and Fun Romance Box Collection
Beating Hades' Bikers

Watch for more at www.lexytimms.com.

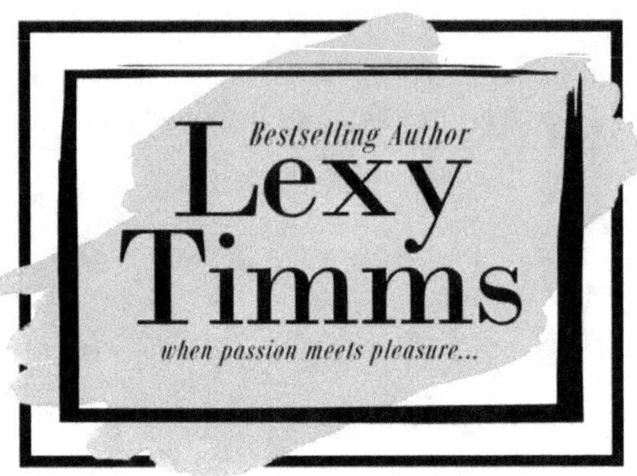

About the Author

"Love should be something that lasts forever, not is lost forever." Visit USA TODAY BESTSELLING AUTHOR, LEXY TIMMS https://www.facebook.com/SavingForever *Please feel free to connect with me and share your comments. I love connecting with my readers.* Sign up for news and updates and freebies - I like spoiling my readers! http://eepurl.com/9i0vD website: www.lexytimms.com Dealing in Antique Jewelry and hanging out with her awesome hubby and three kids, Lexy Timms loves writing in her free time. MANAGING THE BOSSES is a bestselling 10-part series dipping into the lives of Alex Reid and Jamie Connors. Can a secretary really fall for her billionaire boss?

Read more at www.lexytimms.com.